HUSH LOVE 2

HUSH LOVE 2

By

Jordan Belcher

LiT is Officially Here!

Text **LEO SULLIVAN** to

22828

to join our mailing list! To submit a
manuscript for our review, email us
at
submissions@leolsullivan.com

Felony Books, a division of Olive Group, LLC,
P.O. Box 1577, Belton, MO 64012

ISBN-13: 978-1542542319

Felony Books 1st edition January 2017

10 9 8 7 6 5 4 3 2 1

Manufactured in the United States of America

For information regarding special discounts for bulk purchases, please contact Felony Books at felonybooks@gmail.com.

Books by Jordan Belcher

STATUS
STATUS 2
STATUS 3
SELFIE
TRE POUND
TRE POUND 2
TRE POUND 3
BLACKTOP HUSTLAZ
HUSH LOVE

www.jordanbelcher.com

Chapter 1

Irving Mercee, *Cocaine Kingpin*

"You seen Nysha?" I ask Eric, as I climb up on the lip of one of the dock doors in the rear of the B.N.I. building. Eric is on a forklift, hauling a load off the trailer of a docked 18-wheeler.

"Yeah, she's around here somewhere," he says. "You might wanna stay away from her, though. She's been in a bad mood all day."

"Why?"

"Man, I don't know." He shrugs. "You know women. It could be anything."

I walk up the ramp alongside his forklift. "I don't wanna roam all around this building looking for her. I'm supposed to be off today. Where'd you see her last?"

"She was out in the warehouse scanning boxes all over the building for some reason. No telling where she is now. But if I was you, I'd check her office first."

"Okay, thanks."

"What's in the box?" he asks.

Under my arm is a cardboard package sealed with Mexican flag-styled wrapping tape. "It's a souvenir for Nysha," I say.

"Oh, that's right. You took off to go to Mexico. Where's *my* gift?"

I laugh. "You ain't my supervisor. I don't have to kiss up to you."

He laughs with me. "But you could've brought me back a brick of that pure white shit, you stingy-ass nigga. I know you don't hustle no more, but I do. And I know you still got connections down there. You could've hooked a brotha up. I'm tired of this job. This shit ain't me."

"If I was still in the game, I'd fuck wit' you, but ..." I lift my shoulders, keep them up. "I can't help you, brotha. I'm living a different life now. Gotta respect it."

Eric sucks his teeth, then asks, "When are you coming back to work?"

"I'll be here tomorrow. Why?"

"Oh, I didn't see your name on the schedule none this week, or next week."

"Really?"

"Check it yourself to be sure, but I didn't see you on there."

That's odd, I think to myself.

Out of curiosity, I stop by the main bulletin board to

check out the schedule for the week. And just as Eric said, my name is nowhere on it. Not this week, next week, or any of the weeks thereafter. Normally, if there's some kind of major change in my hours Nysha would call me ahead of time.

There has to be some kind of a mistake.

I go inside Nysha's office, shut her door quietly. She's sitting at her desk, reading paperwork. I can't see her face because the side of her head is resting on her fist.

"Hey there," I say, smiling.

She doesn't even look up at me. "Hello."

"Where's the love? Is this how you treat a man who comes bearing gifts?"

I hold out my package. When she doesn't acknowledge it, I gently set it on her desk. Then I step back and cross my arms, waiting to see her reaction. I'm trying to keep from breaking into a smile. Inside is a set of dinnerware hand-painted in Mexican folk art. I couldn't get her expensive jewelry like I did Brandi because of obvious reasons, but Nysha is a more "thought that counts" type of person anyway.

"You're gonna love me even more after you see what it is," I say.

But Nysha doesn't even reach for the box. She keeps reading.

"Quit being a workaholic and pay attention to what I just put in front of you, young lady."

Nysha finally touches the box—but only to push it to the edge of her desk, out of her way. She grabs another sheet of paperwork and looks over it.

I frown. "You're not gonna open it?"

"No, I'm not. Can't you see I'm busy?"

I sit down on her desk, literally planting my backside right on top of her documents. I snatch the paper she's reading out of her hands. "I'll take this," I say playfully. And then I open up the box right in front of her face, folding the cardboard flaps back.

She has no choice but to stare at the artistic Hispanic culture on the clay plates inside.

"This is for you," I say. "For being there for me. For looking out for me. I know you like this type of stuff. It's all hand-made."

"I don't want it," she replies.

I give her a sour look. I think about what Eric just told me. *She's been in a bad mood all day,* he'd said. But there's been plenty of times she's been upset with the world, at everybody at work—everybody but me. *Never* me. So I'm starting to get worried.

I hardly ever flat-out ask women what's wrong with them when I know for sure they're pissed, because it can make the situation worse. I always keep poking until it comes out voluntarily.

"It's a gift from me to you," I say to her. "You don't have to want it, but you have to at least accept it."

"Thanks, but no thanks."

"Okay. If I sell these plates online, I'm probably gonna end up doing something stupid with the proceeds, like make it rain at the strip club. You don't want that, do you?"

"Oh, I'm sure you're not worried about wasting money."

"I am too. Especially since I'm not on the work schedule at all."

She looks at me finally, and I see a consuming anger in her eyes I've never seen before. "You know why you're not on the schedule, don't you?"

I'm almost afraid to ask. "No, why?"

"Because you're fired," she says.

The word "fired" rings in my head consistently for a moment, but I'm so worried about the source of Nysha's pain that it takes a minute for me to realize what this means. I can't be fired. Not *now*. I just made one of the biggest drug deals of my life, and if I'm not here on the ground floor to make sure Jose Horrell's cocaine gets distributed to the right cities, then not only will I be losing millions of dollars, but it could also start a war.

I rack my brain, trying to figure out which manager I pissed off.

"Did Justin fire me?" I ask her.

"No."

"Was it Bryan? He find out you gave me extra paid days off?"

"No."

"Who canned me then?"

"I did it, Mercee!" Nysha says fiercely. "I fired you, because you're a lying motherfucker!"

Her emotion cuts me to the core. And when I see tears well up in her eyes, my forehead wrinkles with sympathy, my helper-instincts searching her face for the source of all of her frustration. *Where is this coming from? What could I have done?* I have no clue.

"What did ...?"

She cuts me off. "What did you do? You don't know what you did? You know damn well what you did. So you tell me."

"I don't know, that's why I'm asking."

"Oh, you know."

"Did Eric tell you some more bullshit about Brandi, or some other female from my past?"

"It's not about your past, Mercee. It's about the shit you're involved in *right now*."

She shows me what she's been reading. I lean close, squinting at the list. It's a printout of shipping and receiving items dating all the way back to when I first started working here. My heart starts beating faster when I see that every input in the "destination" column has the same city/state— Juarez, Mexico, all the way down the sheet.

I look at her. She stares back, wanting an explanation.

I play dumb. "I fucked up that many orders?"

She jumps to her feet, pointing her finger in my face. "You're a piece of shit, you know that? You haven't changed. You're still the same fucking criminal you used to be."

"Nysha, calm down. I don't know what you're talking about." But I do know. I'm trying to figure out how she found out.

"Oh really? So I guess all of that fucking cocaine and money that came off of a pallet in your zone belongs to somebody else, huh?"

I really don't know what to say to her. *She knows.* But why haven't the police stormed in to arrest me?

"Nysha—"

"Save it. I just need you to get out of my office and off the premises immediately. You're no longer an employee here at Black Nile Industries."

I rise off of her desk. "What did you do with the cocaine and the money?"

"So it *is* yours?" she asks knowingly.

I don't reply.

"It's been at my house for the last two days," she says. "Because who knows what would've happened if security or somebody higher up found it in the warehouse. You're so fucking stupid, Mercee, *my God.* I thought Eric was the dumbest drug dealer I ever met. Nope, you take the cake."

"When can I pick it up?"

"You can come pick it up after I get off work, along with the rest of your clothes and shit you left over there."

I start for the door, still wondering why she didn't call the police on me. She could've reported this right after she put all the pieces together. But she didn't. Why? I stop and turn back toward her. "Thank you, Nysha, for not ratting me out."

"Fuck you," she spews.

Chapter 2

Nysha Hawk, *Manager*

I hear Irving Mercee knocking on my door—*tap, tap, tap*—
as I'm dragging his plastic tote across my carpeted living
room into the hallway. This tote is heavy as hell, almost
impossible to drag (I didn't realize he had this much stuff
over here), but the hallway has hardwood flooring so when I
cross the threshold I'm able to push the tote and let it slide
across the sheen finish.

I'm perspiring and breathing hard. "Dammit," I curse.
"Why did I let him get this comfortable?"

I pause for a moment, hands on my hips to catch my
breath. On top of the tote is his drugs and his money, still in
their original B.N.I. boxes. I re-sealed them with new pack-
ing tape.

He knocks again.

I grimace. *Is he rushing me?* I would have made him pack his own shit, but I don't want him to set another foot inside my house.

I open my front door. "Everything's right here," I say to him, pointing to the plastic tote. "Your shirts, all your pants, and socks, even the stuff I bought you because I'm not petty. These boxes on top have your cash and your drugs. Please get them far-far away from here."

"May I come in and talk?" he asks nicely.

"No. Get your shit and go."

I notice he's dressed a little bit different than what I'm used to. He has on a vintage linen shirt cuffed to the elbows, which makes the gold Rolex watch on his wrist pop out at you. I've never seen him wear jewelry before, especially not a real Rolex. When he's not in his work khakis, he usually comes over my house in a plain tee and sweats. The most I've ever seen him wearing as far as accessories is a rubberband around his wrist. So this Rolex makes me think he's trying to show off to me. Impress me.

It's not working.

"I won't take up too much of your time," he says. "I just wanna come in and explain myself to you."

"I don't let criminals in my house."

His eyes narrow at me. "That's all I am to you now? A criminal?"

Honestly, I still have the same feelings for him burning through me as I did before I found out he was selling his drugs through B.N.I. But that's just my heart—my vulnerable, naive, stupid heart—unwilling to separate from this man that I've grown to love. My heart prevented me from calling the police on him. My heart convinced me to transport his drugs and money out of the warehouse and bring them here where I knew they'd be safe.

But I'm done following my heart. I have to be smart from here on out.

"Yes, that's all you are to me is a criminal," I state. "And a liar. And a thief."

"Thief?"

"Yes, a thief. I went through the system at B.N.I. and found that you've been cancelling out orders on packages that come into the country from Juarez, Mexico. When you cancel the orders out, the company doesn't get paid. That's stealing! You probably thought you were covering your tracks, but all you were doing was bringing attention to yourself. What do you think was going to happen at the end-of-year audit when the B.N.I. accountants find out they have orders missing? You're lucky I caught it before they did."

He looks surprised. He says, "Can we sit down and talk?"

"I said no. You're not allowed inside my—"

He walks into me and I don't move, so he squeezes past.

I have the urge to snatch him by the neck of his swanky shirt and throw him back out. But he's here. And I really want to know why he betrayed my trust.

I cross my arms, not moving to sit down anywhere.

"I can understand why you're upset," he says. "I told some lies, I broke some rules. But don't just push me out of your life completely."

"Why shouldn't I?"

"Because other than my side hustle, everything else that I've told you about me and my feelings for you are true."

"You call moving hundreds of thousands of dollars—*millions*, maybe—in cocaine through a worldwide distribution company a side hustle? Really, Mercee?"

"It's a side hustle to *me*. That's not my life, it's not my main concern. *You're* my main concern."

"Oh really?"

"Yes, really. Where do I spend all my free time? Here. After work, before work, I'm trying to spend all my time with you. Right *here*."

"Don't give me that. You're not here all the time. There's plenty of times I have no idea where you are and I can't get in touch with you. That should've told me right there that something was wrong. You've been living a double life." I blink a few times, trying to hold back tears. "I guess I'm not enough, huh? All that shit you told me about living a normal, simple life was bullshit. You wanna be a dope dealer. You *are* a dope dealer."

"Temporarily."

"What the hell does that mean?"

"I'm not gonna move drugs forever. I didn't plan on doing it this long. I had hoped to be done with it before you found out. But my plans got extended."

I have no idea what he's trying to sell me, but this whole situation is so confusing and hurtful and unfair. He grabs my wrist and leads me to my couch, where he sits me down with him against my will (sort of). He's holding my hand; I'm not holding his.

"I told you my fiancée got killed while I was in prison. That's what got me back into the drug-dealing mindset," he explains. "Zaki found out that a rival drug-dealer named Don Corey, the new kingpin in Kansas City, killed her to send me a message. Don Corey was letting me know what would happen to me if I tried to take over the city again when I got out."

"I thought you didn't know who killed her."

"I didn't know for sure at the time. I was consumed by rage when I first got out. I had to find a job to stay free, so when you got me hired at B.N.I. and I found out how the company operated, I took the opportunity. My whole plan was to move enough drugs through B.N.I. to take Don Corey's clientele and cripple his revenue stream, and also make enough money to pay people off to find out his whereabouts."

"So you've been doing all of this in the name of revenge?"

He nods. "Yes."

But I look at his Rolex watch skeptically. "Not to buy fancy jewelry?"

He lets go of my hand, unsnaps the watch from his wrist and tosses it on my coffee table. "That shit don't mean nothing to me, Nysha. I'm doing this for someone that I loved, someone that loved me. I'd do the same for you."

"But I don't want that to be me." I jump to my feet, looking down at him. "You want me to overlook the fact that you're a drug dealer? I can't! I'm sorry, I don't wanna end up like Lucille."

"You won't. I won't let that happen."

"How can you promise me that? Are you gonna stop dealing?"

"Yes."

"Right now? Today?"

He hesitates. "I can't."

"Why? Because of your pride? Even after you take over this Don guy's territory, what do you think he's gonna do? Just let you go about your business? No, he's gonna try to kill you and everybody else you know. He's already proved he'll do it."

"Not if he's already dead."

I blink once, as it becomes very clear that all the horror stories that Eric told me about Mercee are all true. The way Mercee just spoke of taking Don Corey's life, how easily it flowed from his lips, is a piercing reality check that I've been sharing my heart with a cold-blooded murderer.

But for some reason I still feel safe with him in this room.

"It's not only about revenge at this particular point," he says. "I just made a deal with my supplier that I have to see through."

"That's what you went to Mexico to do?"

"Yes."

"What happens if you just walk away?"

"I'll have a price to pay. It could be a dollar amount for all the inconvenience I caused, or my supplier could put a price on my head. He's already taking a chance on me because I'm fresh out of prison; I'm hot, technically, so for me to renege on our deal, it'll be a big problem."

"How long will it take you to fulfill your end of the bargain?"

"About six months," he says. "So I need my job back, Nysha, just for a little bit longer."

I let out a derisive laugh. "That's not gonna happen. Especially if you think you're gonna handle those shipments like you've been doing. The end-of-year audit is in three months, so you'll be in federal prison by month five. You can look at all of the paperwork yourself."

I leave the room and go get the file folder out of my workbag. I come back and hand him the folder.

"Is this what you showed me earlier?" he asks, looking at the printouts inside.

"Yes, and more. You left a paper trail, Mercee, a long fucking trail of bread crumbs that leads directly back to packages handled on your shift. The evidence is right there in your hand. If you were a smart drug dealer, you would have deleted all of the transactions from Juarez, Mexico, out of the B.N.I. system *completely*, not just canceled the orders. And at the very least, you wouldn't have scheduled the cocaine packages to arrive at the warehouse only on the days you work. You were asking for an indictment."

He's scrutinizing the pages, seeing exactly what I'm talking about. "I never knew that the shipments could be entirely removed from the system," he says. "I thought as long as I kept a package's contents unlisted, then the worst that would happen was the package would display a 'system error' code and, because the shipping coordinates were valid, it'd still get pushed through successfully. I thought I had my bases covered."

"You thought wrong."

He reads some more, then looks at me and says, "So if the cops suspect that I'm moving dope through B.N.I., all they have to do is print this off and they pretty much got me?"

"That's what would have happened, yes."

He appears confused. "Would have?"

"The entries are no longer there. I deleted them."

His eyebrows go up. "You what?"

"I've been breaking rules for you since you started

working there, Mercee. I hate you for lying to me, but I still don't want to see you go back to prison."

"You still love me?"

"Yes, I still love you. But I'm not breaking the rules for you anymore. That was my last time."

"I don't need you to break the rules for me anymore. Just give me my job back, let me finish out my deal with my connect and I'm done. Can you do that for me? Please?"

I rub my forehead, trying to ease the headache he's giving me.

"Six more months," he pleads. "That's all I ask."

I wish there was another way. I wish me and Mercee could just go back to being secret boyfriend and girlfriend and this drug predicament never happened. I liked kissing him in the break room when no one was looking, knowing if we got caught our jobs would be in jeopardy. But with this cocaine moving through B.N.I., it won't just be about our jobs—our very *freedom* will be on the line.

Chapter 3

Abe Gholson, *President of B.N.I.*

I didn't think much about taking time out of my day to speak with detectives about one of my employees being involved in a crime or criminal activity. I lose hundreds of employees annually—some find better jobs, others get fired for poor work performance, and a lot end up in jail because of offenses perpetrated in their free time and sometimes on our grounds. And when I say *hundreds*, that's just here at B.N.I.'s Kansas City warehouse, what we call "World Headquarters." But we have warehouses all over the nation, in every state. Tens of thousands of employees and affiliates in the United States, with smaller warehouses abroad. So I was surprised that my accountant said that this particular criminal, Irving Mercee, could pose a problem. What makes this asshole so special to me?

"He's not your everyday perpetrator. He's a drug king-pin," my accountant, Nicholas Rolfe, tells me from his seat across from my desk. The Jewish 62-year-old CPA takes his prescription glasses off, cleans off a smudge with a handkerchief. "His record consists of one federal arrest and conviction, the result of a 4-year criminal investigation. The detectives coming to visit you today, Detectives Frisk and Copeland, are the officers who took him down seven years ago. Mr. Irving Mercee has only been free about a year and has just recently been released from parole."

"But still," I say, "we've had tons of idiots that try to use our services illegally. How can this one guy hurt my company?"

Nick Rolfe puts his specs back on. "Two ways. The first is through public relations, if we don't get a handle on it at the jump. And by handle, I suggest putting a gag order on the detectives coming to visit you today. We don't want them speaking to the media about B.N.I. being unknown participants in the trafficking of illegal narcotics."

"I'll make sure the detectives sign paperwork ensuring that our conversation today stays confidential. What's the second way this can hurt us?"

"We're not certain how much drugs this Irving Mercee fellow has been moving through our warehouse, if any at all—mind you, this is just detectives coming to ask questions; they're probably not certain of anything. But if Mr. Mercee has been active in using our facilities as his personal drug hub, then the consequences to us depends on how much he's been pushing through our system. I found documentation in his previous case that proves he's capable of moving tons of cocaine across the country. With the distribution services we provide here, there's no limit to the amount of drugs he can move. A ton of cocaine parceled out into individual packages can travel to all 50 states in a matter of hours with the efficiency of our carriers."

I laugh at Nick. "You gotta be kidding me. This is all hypothetical, right? You don't really think this one guy can figure out how to sneak that much cocaine through B.N.I., do you?"

"Actually, I do."

Nick lays his briefcase across his lap, clicking it open. He removes a file folder and hands it to me. I give a cursory glance to each sheet of reports inside.

"You're looking at the daily stock data from earlier this year, when Irving Mercee first started working here," says Nick. "The rapid rise in our stocks coincides with Mercee's start date. There's a possibility that his illegal business dealings has positively effected our growth."

I do a quick calculation in my head, coming up with an estimated total sum of the ending balances on each report. "So you mean to tell me that Mr. Mercee, an hourly wage forklift driver, has made me about thirty-five million dollars in less than a year?"

"Yes, but I'm also telling you that if Mr. Mercee is prosecuted, then his drug-generated business departs along with him, and our stock prices will subsequently drop. And factoring in the public scandal that will likely ensue, it could cause our stocks to plummet sharply. It could end up costing B.N.I. *billions*."

"That's unacceptable." I lean forward, starting to take this conversation more serious. "What do you suggest we do? If we fire him, we're still gonna lose money."

"Our payroll says he's already been terminated."

My eyebrows raise. "When?"

"Yesterday."

"Holy shit. What did he get fired for?"

"Apparently he's had one absence too many."

Nick hands me another sheet of paper, an obligatory legal record of termination that every manager has to fill out when an employee is let go. I read the reason for termination; it simply states: "abuse of absence." There's no detailed description of accumulated violations, which is unusual. So I scan back up the page to the name of the manager who filled out this report.

Nysha Hawk.

The name strikes a sensitive cord within me, causing a reverberation of mixed emotions to tingle throughout my whole body. I used to date Nysha Hawk. I thought I was falling in love with her (as silly as that sounds). But she dumped me when she found out I was having sex with several other of my employees.

"So if he's fired, what options do we have now?" I ask.

"I think we need to do our own internal investigation," Nick says. "No cooperation with law enforcement until we can figure out exactly what Irving Mercee has done under our noses."

"So I need to reschedule the meeting with Detectives Frisk and Copeland?"

"No, you need to talk to them as soon as possible to find out what they know. Probe them. But don't give them any information on how B.N.I. operates in return. If we reveal nothing, they know nothing, reducing the chances of them giving the media a story to run with, whether they sign a gag order or not."

"Okay. Thanks, Nick."

"No problem. That's my job. And there's no need to get worked up over this. There's still hope that the problem isn't as bad as it seems."

"But you know me—I don't make decisions based off intangibles such as *hope*. I wouldn't be where I'm at today, operating a billion-dollar enterprise, if I relied on *hope*. No, I make things happen and I make things go away."

"As you should, sir." Nick gives me a farewell nod, packs up his briefcase and heads out.

I lean back in my chair, musing about this criminal, Irving Mercee. Right now he's in limbo with me, because according to Nick's theory, Mr. Mercee could have very well made me money so far—to the tune of thirty-five mill. But after factoring in the risk of potentially losing billions behind this drug pusher, the odds are overwhelmingly against me.

And I'm not a gambling man. I either win, or I take.

I roll out my keyboard and access the B.N.I. database, typing in Irving Mercee's name in the search box. His profile pops up, listed as "No Longer Assigned." I click the thumbnail, expanding it to the edges of my screen. He's exactly what I expected to see—blank stare, facial hair groomed, piercing eyes, tattoos rippling up his neck, and sporting a company collar shirt, B.N.I. badge stitched to his chest. He looks like a street dealer, not a kingpin.

I feel a little bit more relieved.

Turning to my desk phone, I dial HR.

"Human resources, this is Imani," a woman answers.

"Imani, I need you to send Nysha Hawk to my office."

"Who am I speaking with?"

"Abe Gholson."

"Oh, hello, Mr. Gholson. I'll page her right now."

"Thank you."

A few minutes after I hang up, Imani calls me back and tells me that Nysha's shift is over and she'll be back tomorrow morning. Imani promises to make sure Nysha sees me first thing.

To jog my memory, I take out my cell phone and scroll through my internal photo gallery until I find a picture of me and Nysha together. It was taken, selfie-style, at dinner in the Power and Light District. I remember now what type of girl she was—reserved, full of self-respect (too much), and she reeked of that girl-power shit. The only good qualities she had was her looks and her body. I remember having to pretend to be a gentleman for a long time in order to sleep with her.

I pinch my screen and zoom in on her face. *God, she's beautiful,* I say to myself. *Why the hell did I let her get away from me?* Suddenly, I'm anxious to talk to her about more than just Irving Mercee.

Chapter 4

Nysha Hawk, *Manager*

I've never been this nervous in my life.

Coffee didn't help me this morning. It only loosened my bowels, sending me to the toilet twice. I tried breathing exercises before I left the house, but I'm still jittery as I pull into my reserved parking spot at Black Nile Industries.

I don't see how drug dealers can live like this. I haven't even really done anything wrong yet, and my conscience is tearing me apart.

I notice a KCPD squad car parked several cars down from me, its wheels turned crookedly, as if it zoomed in here and parked, as if the officers hopped out and ran in the warehouse. To get who? I start thinking the worst—*they're here to take you to jail, Nysha. Why did you let Mercee talk you into doing this? Now you're a criminal just like him.*

I shake off the thoughts and steel myself against them, as I walk inside the building. Everything seems normal so far, a few co-workers waving to me, no one staring, just normal everyday production. I head to the breakroom to heat up my breakfast croissant.

Upon entering, I see Eric handing another employee a bag of marijuana—his umpteenth drug deal on B.N.I. property. With so much going on these last few days, I lose it.

"Give it here, NOW!" I yell at the guy who I watched sit on the bag in a poor attempt to hide it. His name is Ben, if I remember correctly. He used Eric as a reference to get hired here. He reaches under himself, grabs the bag of weed and hands it to me.

Eric tries to leave the breakroom but I grab his arm. I squeeze as hard as I can.

"Oouw!" Eric squeals. "Dammit, Nysha, that shit hurts!"

"Both of you idiots are fired!" I yell. I look at the buyer, Ben. "And you haven't even been working here long. Sucks that you let Eric get you fired before you're even done with your probationary period."

Eric tries to pull free, but I don't let him go. "Don't fire me, Nysha," he begs. "I was just getting rid of the last of my stash. I'm done. I'm sorry."

"You're right, you *are* done." I shove him toward the door. "Get out of here. And take your buddy with you. I've given you too many chances and you keep trying me. Get out! And turn in your uniforms or it's getting deducted from your last checks."

Eric knows I'm serious this time. He storms out and slams the breakroom door. The newbie, Eric's buyer, gathers his food, tosses it in the trash and leaves next, without saying a word to me.

I stick my breakfast croissant in the microwave, letting out a huge sigh. The irony hits me—*I just fired two people for doing the same thing that I'm about to re-hire Mercee to do.*

My heart starts beating fast again.

I take my food and head to my office, plop down at my desk. I look at my croissant and realize I don't even have an appetite. Powering on my computer, I key in my password and immediately start typing in the reason for Eric's termination, as well as Ben's. "Possession of an illegal substance on B.N.I. property." I know it's hypocritical. But I can't have Eric slanging drugs all around here, creating unnecessary attention, while I'm trying to help Mercee move his packages through the system for the next six months.

I pull up Mercee's profile on my screen.

With the click of a button, I have the power to make his status go from "No Longer Assigned" to "Assigned." *But should I do this?* It hasn't even been a full 48 hours since I removed him, so I'm pretty sure no one has even noticed that he's been unassigned. Yes, I filled out a record of termination, but if approached about it I can easily explain it away as me being misinformed about his off days. I can claim it was a computer error.

In my head, my conscience and my heart are vying for attention: *Don't be stupid!* my conscience shouts. *You're putting your life on the line for an ex-con. When did you start doing dumb shit like this?* But my heart has a more soothing approach. *He's not just an ex-con,* it whispers. *He's a man you fell in love with, a man you gave your heart to. Sometimes we have to step outside of our comfort zone to extend help to the ones we care about.*

I take another deep breath, as my finger hovers over the "enter" key. I'm a click away from aiding and abetting a drug kingpin.

I nearly jump out of my seat when I hear my name over the warehouse loudspeaker:

"Nysha Hawk to Human Resources. Nysha Hawk to Human Resources."

Panic burns inside my chest. My breathing comes faster, my lungs working doubletime. *Why does HR want me?* I wonder, deliriously. Then I have a moment of clarity, realizing that I just fired two people. *This has nothing to do with Irving Mercee,* I reassure myself. *It's just Eric or Ben, pissed off, filing a complaint against me, something every other employee does to get their job back.*

I head to the Human Resources department, planting my forearms on the counter. I show my best smile.

"Hi, I'm Nysha Hawk. Floor manager. I was called over here for some reason."

The HR lady's nametag reads: Bobbi. "Hey, Nysha, you got a very special call today," Bobbi says merrily.

My smile disappears. "From who?"

"The head boss himself. Abe Gholson."

"Abe?"

"Yes. He requested to see you as soon as your shift started. He's ready for you now."

"Thanks, Bobbi."

I'm wringing my hands as I make my way to the other end of the warehouse, where the corporate offices are located. I haven't been in Abe's office since me and him broke up, which was no less than two years ago, long before me and Mercee started dating.

I knock on his door, three quick raps.

I hear his deep sand-paper voice tell me to come in, so I do, shutting the door behind me. I stay close to the door for some reason, maybe because I feel safer nearest an exit.

He waves me closer. "Sit down, Nysha. How can I talk to you way back there?"

Taking a deep breath, I walk over and sit down in a leather arm chair. He's sitting across from me at his desk, wearing a light blue button-up, no jacket. He's staring at me the way he used to whenever he was ready to have sex— and it's giving me the creeps. I notice that he's purchased him a new pinky ring; this one is diamond-encrusted like his former one, but bigger. *Still flashy and conceited,* I say to myself. And as much as hate to admit it, he's also just as handsome as he's always been. His skin is flawlessly jet black, the darkest man I've ever dated. I remember running my hands over his chiseled, naked body, fascinated by how his deep complexion brings out the definition in his muscles.

If only he hadn't been a total asshole.

"You requested to see me?" I say.

"Yes." He fondles his chin hair. "I have a problem ..."

"Did I do something wrong?"

"No. You can do no wrong, you know that."

I don't want to respond to that, so I don't.

"The problem pertains to an employee that worked in your department."

My skin starts to tingle.

"Which one?" I ask nervously.

"Irving Mercee," he says.

No oxygen—it all just left the room. My head feels fuzzy.

"Nysha, you okay?" he asks.

I swallow the lump in my throat. "Yes, I'm fine," I say, adjusting myself in my seat. "Irving Mercee. The name kinda rings a bell."

"It should. You just fired him."

"Oh okay. Yes, him. Irving Mercee." I adjust myself again. "I let him go because he was taking too many days off."

"Yeah, I read your report. But the strange thing about it is that there were no violations leading up to his termination. Normally there's a paper trail. Why is there not one with him?"

Because Mercee's my boyfriend, and I made sure no write-ups stuck to his file. I feel stupid for doing that now.

"I don't know," comes out my mouth.

"What?"

"I ... He ... He was a good employee. At least I thought he was, so I overlooked a lot of his minor wrongs, little things like showing up a few minutes late or clocking out early. But when I learned the truth about who he really was—a liar, who had been taking unauthorized days off—I felt justified in terminating him immediately."

He nods, believing me—*I think*. "Can you keep a secret?" he asks.

"Excuse me?"

He laughs. "Who am I kidding? Of course you can keep a secret. You kept our relationship a secret, still haven't told a soul, have you?"

"No, I haven't." *Why would I tell anybody I dated a self-centered, lying, cheating pig that slept with every pretty face that walked through B.N.I.'s doors, a jerk that had the audacity to claim I was selfish for walking away and retaining my dignity and self-respect—*

"The man you fired, Irving Mercee, is under investigation for drug trafficking," he says in the middle of my silent rant, and I'm suddenly scared to death. "Authorities believe he's been moving his drugs through the B.N.I. warehouse somehow. My question to you is: Did you see or notice anything suspicious about him before you fired him? Did you catch him tampering with any packages? Did you see him logging into our system, changing codes?"

"No," I say quickly. "If I would have caught him doing any of that stuff, I would have fired him on the spot."

"Whenever he took time off, did he give you reasoning? Were they sick days? Was he vacationing? Did he say where he was going, in or out of the country?"

His questions are coming too fast. All I can do is lie. "No," I say. "I don't know what he did in his free time."

"I can see you're flustered," Abe points out. "You're not in any trouble. You do a great job here, always have. It's just that I have a meeting with two detectives this morning. Actually, they're waiting on me in the conference room right now, but I needed to talk to you first in order to get some more information on this guy."

"I'm sorry I couldn't be of more help."

"You helped a lot. I know how organized you are. You're aware of what the people under you are doing. You pay a lot of attention to detail. So I'm sure if Irving Mercee was doing something under our noses, you would have caught it. These detectives seem to think this guy is some kind of intelligent kingpin, but I'm starting to think they're full of it, probably wasting my time."

"Is that all you needed from me?"

"Yep, that's it."

He's giving me that look again, his creepy sex stare. I get up and head for the door. He lifts himself out of his seat and follows, showing me out.

He touches my arm, and I look back at him with a cross face. "How's your mom doing?" he asks.

From experience, I know this question is manipulative. Abe never asked about my mother. Whenever I talked about her and her cigarette-related medical issues, he'd act bored, playing on his phone, or he'd cut me off mid-sentence to ask what color I thought his next Rolls-Royce should be.

"She's doing better," I answer.

"If she needs any money for hospital bills, all you have to do is ask."

"Thanks for offering, but she's fine. She's insured."

I turn to leave and I feel his fingers graze the back of my hand, as if he wants to hold hands. I pull away, but he manages to make a full fist around my pinky finger. I yank it free.

"What are you doing?" I snap.

"Call me some time," he smiles.

I leave his office. And when I finally get to mine, I lock the door and call Mercee.

Chapter 5

Michael Frisk, *Detective*

"What's taking this nigga so long?" Copeland asks, swiveling side to side in a high-back leather chair at the head of the oak conference room table. I tried to tell him to sit in one of the smaller leather chairs on either side of the table, like me, but he wanted the "Executive" chair.

"Copeland, this man is the President of B.N.I.," I say. "I'm sure he has a lot more important matters to attend to first."

"What's more important than us? We're the fucking police, investigating a drug-dealing, murdering psychopath."

"Copeland, all Mr. Gholson knows is that one of his employees *might* have committed a crime. Put yourself in his shoes—you're a rich business man with thousands upon thousands of employees. I'm sure half of them have had trouble with the law. This is nothing new to him. We're probably inconveniencing him as it is. So don't exacerbate the situation by having an attitude."

Copeland just keeps swiveling. He doesn't break a smile until he finds out that his chair has adjustable lumbar support. "You see this shit?" he cheeses at me, as if I care. "Damn, I wish we could confiscate this."

My partner, bless his soul, is wearing a lightweight army-green jacket, its hood pulled up over his head with the drawstrings hanging down past his shoulders. The hood is so encompassing, it casts a shadow down his face. I can only see his mouth. Compared to how professional I'm dressed—cotton button-up, slacks, dress shoes—one would think I was a criminal lawyer representing my client. But I can't complain too much about how my partner is dressed. He suited up when it counted, in Chief Knam's office the other day. He helped re-open the Irving Mercee case. He got us here. *So, for now—wear what you want, Copeland.*

The double doors to the conference room push open. Me and Copeland turn and look, both standing up when we see Mr. Abe Gholson walking toward us, his hand extended. There's an old white man with him, a briefcase tucked under his arm.

"Sorry to keep you gentlemen waiting," says Mr. Gholson, shaking my hand. He turns, gives Copeland's attire a curious expression, then shakes his hand too. "Undercover?" he asks him.

"No," Copeland says. "This is my everyday lockup-bad-guys wear."

"Good to hear," says Abe. "Now if you can please step away from my seat, I'd be glad to get started."

Copeland glances at the fancy chair one last time before dropping into a seat next to me. "I didn't know we had assigned seats," he grumbles.

After everyone is seated, the old man introduces himself as Nicholas Rolfe. He sets his briefcase on the table, clicks it open and takes out a small digital recorder. He centers it on the table. "All legal proceedings that take place on B.N.I. property have to be recorded," he explains.

It's not our department's practice to consent to a recording, but I don't have much to say so I get right down to business. "First off, thank you guys for agreeing to speak with us. We believe that one of your employees is moving a large amount of cocaine through your warehouse and we want to do everything we can to stop him."

"Irving Mercee, correct?" asks Nicholas Rolfe.

"Yes," I say.

"And how did you reach this conclusion?"

"We received an anonymous tip."

"A tip, that's it? So basically this claim holds very little merit?"

Copeland pushes his hood off his head, then leans forward with his forearms on the table. He has a five-o-clock shadow. "Every tip we pursue has *merit*," he says. "We don't chase every single lead we come across. Is that what you think we do all day? This particular tip contained audio of Irving Mercee himself saying he pushes his drugs through B.N.I. So this is a self-incriminating tip."

"Has his voice already been verified by a competent audio forensics expert?" the Rolfe guy asks.

"Has your hairpiece been approved by animal rights—?"

I kick Copeland's leg under the table before he can finish, then I take the floor. "No, Mr. Rolfe, the audio we received hasn't been authenticated. But that's not an issue because myself and Detective Copeland here know his voice, we know his speech pattern, we know it's Irving Mercee. There's no doubt in my mind that an audio forensics expert will succeed in proving it's him on the tape, when that time comes. But right now we'd just like to get an idea of how Irving Mercee might be using your services to traffic his drugs. Do all employees have access to your internal database, tracking, shipping coordinates?"

Abe Gholson joins the conversation. "No," he says flatly. "Only managers have that kind of access. If Irving Mercee somehow found out how to tap into our system, one of our managers would have caught it by now."

"He's very intelligent," I point out.

"So am I," Abe replies. "Throughout the years, I've applied many safeguards to B.N.I.'s system. Our managers are highly trained in anti-theft and illegal distribution. Before becoming a manager, employees have to go through a 4-week course that includes crime-prevention and American law. It's drummed into their heads over and over. They know what to watch for and how to prevent this very thing from happening. There's no way Irving Mercee could operate inside of this warehouse. Maybe those folks down the street, but not here."

"You're putting a lot of emphasis and trust in your managers. Is it possible that Mercee could have secured a manager's passcodes, or somehow influenced one of them? Paid them off, maybe?"

Abe shakes his head no. "Our managers are compensated very well. No drug dealer can afford to pay my employees what I pay them."

Copeland rubs his forehead, frustrated. "Yes, *Irving Mercee can*. He's a kingpin. He has money pouring out of his ears. He owned a Bentley before his 21st birthday."

"Can we speak to Irving Mercee's manager?" I ask.

"We'll have to find out who is manager is," says Nicholas Rolfe, "and then we'll have to get back with you."

"His manager is Nysha Hawk," I say.

Abe Gholson looks at me with contempt. "And how do you know that?"

"We're intelligent too," Copeland quips.

I sigh, then say, "We obtained information that Mr. Irving Mercee targeted Black Nile Industries specifically, and he knew beforehand that Nysha Hawk was one of the

Jordan Belcher

hiring managers. I'd like to find out from her if he contacted her prior to getting a job here."

"Her name wasn't listed as a reference on his application," Nicholas Rolfe says.

"That's nice to know. But we'd still like to speak with her."

"If you give me 48 hours' notice, we can set that up," Abe agrees. "But first I'd like to know where this information connecting Irving Mercee to Nysha Hawk came from."

"Prison documents," I say. "Irving Mercee spent a lot of time in his cell taking a lot of notes before he decided on B.N.I. He's a very cunning, calculated, patient man. Nysha Hawk may have unwittingly hired the most dangerous criminal to come out of Kansas City in the past 20 years. He's very manipulative, especially with women."

"Nysha Hawk is actually one of the best managers here," Abe says proudly. "I know her personally. She's not one to be manipulated. She's not motivated by money. She's focused on getting the job done. This further affirms my belief that Mr. Irving Mercee was not trafficking drugs through B.N.I."

I narrow my eyes at Abe. "You keep using the word *was*. We're certain that Irving Mercee *is* still active in illegal activity within your business."

"Even more impossible," Abe says with a smile. "Irving Mercee was terminated a few days ago."

I feel insulted. These two rich goofballs had been holding onto this information since the interview started, but chose to wait until now to tell us. Fucking assholes. I had planned to get Abe Gholson's help in setting up an on-the-job sting, catching Mercee *in the act*. But now that he's no longer an employee at B.N.I., I have to re-work my strategy. *Shit.*

I ask Abe if Mercee was canned before or after we contacted his office; Nicholas Rolfe speaks up, tells us *before*. Nysha Hawk allegedly fired him for having too many absences, and she filled out a report documenting it. I request a print-out of the report and Abe says, "I'll see what I can do." I stand, shake their hands again and we all head out of the conference room.

Me and Copeland wind up in the elevator alone, riding down to the lobby in silence.

"We got played," I say after the elevator lets us out. "They got more information out of us than we did out of them."

Copeland nods. "They didn't give us shit to go on."

"They're more worried about protecting their company. And if that means protecting Mercee, then that's what they're gonna do."

"You think Mercee really got fired a few days ago?" Copeland asks me, holding the exit door open for me as we head outside to our squad car. "Or did they fire him after we told them they have a kingpin on their payroll?"

"I can't be certain right now. But I'm hoping that Nysha Hawk can give us some better answers than those two bozos."

"That's *if* they let us talk to her. Who knows when that'll get approved."

"Approval or not, we're talking to her. Sooner rather than later."

I start the car up. And as I drive off, I look up at the larger-than-life B.N.I. marquee on the side of the building. There's also a banner stretched across several glass window panels that reads: "World Headquarters," and on another sign, "Global Distribution, Fast, Reliable." In my gut I know Mercee is—or *was*—using these services to his advantage. He said it out of his own mouth.

And Nysha Hawk. I know she's inside that building somewhere. I'm sure if I asked Copeland, he'd agree to go back inside and knock on doors and ask employees where she was until we found her—or until security kicked us out. But we're walking on too many eggshells with Chief Knam as it is. He wouldn't be too pleased to hear that two of his detectives got thrown out of the #1 distribution company in Kansas City, a company that pays the highest bracket of state taxes that keeps our police department up and running. We'd be in a hellavuh shit storm.

As I turn out of the parking lot, I get a deep sense that we're driving away from so many hidden, helpless clues. *Come back*, I hear them pleading voicelessly. *Frisk, don't leave us here. Come back!*

54

Chapter 6

Brandi Nieman, *Telemarketer*

Mercee mounts me from behind, his bare hands pinning my hips to his bed. Blood pounds in my brain, a symptom of over-pleasure and disorientation jumbled together. *I don't know if I can take another sex position!* my mind screams. His enormous erection digs in my pussy again, slowly, deeply—then settles there, pulsing hot. I clench my whole midsection, gripping him tight, as if to keep his heat in check.

He leans against me. "I just wanna stay right here, snuggled up in you," he whispers, his warm breath tickling the shell of my ear. "Can I stay here?"

"*Yesss,*" I moan.

"No?"

"Baby, *yesss.*"

He gyrates against me, most of his length staying put. "I can't hear you. What?"

"*Mmmm*, keep doin' that."

He does, and after a few moments he finally cums inside of me.

He lets me up. I stuff a towel between my nude legs before his semen has a chance to ooze out onto his bed sheets. "What time is my flight?" I ask him.

He stands by the bed as naked as me, TV remote in hand, clicking through channels to find the news. His meat is hanging long and limp down his thigh. "In about six hours," he replies after he finds his channel. He tosses the remote on the bed. "So you better start getting ready."

"I would've been ready if you didn't rip all of my clothes off when I walked in the door."

"No excuses, slacker."

I watch his tall, brown frame slip away to the bathroom. I eye the big tattoos arching across his back, and the ones circling his calves. Some are old (tats I watched him get when we were teenagers) and some are new (tats he got while in prison). I'm so glad to have him back in my life. We're the old us, but so much better, so much wiser than before.

I listen to him peeing in the toilet.

"Mercee?"

"Yeah?"

I hesitate. "Why do I have to go out of town by myself?"

He flushes the toilet, comes back in the room and sits down next to me again. His eyes are so fucking beautiful. "Because I can't take any more days off work. I damn near got fired for taking that last trip to Mexico. Actually, I *did* get fired. I had to beg my manager for my job back."

"I don't wanna go by myself. In the old days, we always took our trips together."

"This isn't the old days, Brandi."

"I know. But this is my first trip out of town in years. You can at least accompany me to make sure I don't fuck up."

"Why would you fuck up? You know how to talk to customers. You're the perfect salesgirl."

"But we haven't spent a lot of time together," I say. "Why can't Zaki do it this time?"

He gives me a look that says I should already know why he didn't pick Zaki. And I do know. Zaki has no people skills. He's arrogant, selfish, condescending—someone you don't want to be around unless you have to. I've even seen Mercee "take breaks" from him, going weeks without speaking to him; not because he was mad at Zaki, but because Zaki's negativity is overbearing at times.

This Detroit, Michigan, trip I'm taking later feels like a test. Mercee is testing me. I'm supposed to meet a local drug leader there and explain to him the process of shipping and receiving drugs through B.N.I. (a process that only took ten minutes for Mercee to explain to me). The Detroit guys

57

are skeptical, and I have to make them un-skeptical. Simple stuff. No challenge whatsoever. But Mercee wants to know if he can trust me to handle drug business by myself, and since this Detroit meeting is just a tiny drop in his interconnected cocaine ocean, he probably doesn't care whether I secure this deal or not. He wants to know if I still got it. I know I do. I just have to prove to him that I'm a big girl now.

I let out a deep sigh. "Okay, master, I'll go by myself. Your wish is my command."

"I'm not your master," Mercee replies. "We're partners. We've always been partners."

"Partners?" I lay a hand on his penis, gently working my fingers around it, palming it, allowing my thumb to fondle the underside of its head. "That's all? Just partners?"

"That's what you want, ain't it?"

He knows I want more. He knows I want the title that Lucille held. *Fiancée.* And I want the one after that too. *Wife.*

My thumb keeps fondling. His shaft thickens.

"If I make this Detroit deal happen by myself, then when I come back you have to court me."

He laughs. "I have to what?"

"I want a ring."

His dick softens immediately. *I just turned him off.*

"Let's take our time, okay?" he says, kissing me on the lips. "One step at a time. Nature will take its course."

I frown. The last time nature took its course, another girl got the ring and I got stuck with an addiction.

***

As the yellow taxi pulls away from the Wallstreet Towers, I watch Mercee wave goodbye from the sidewalk. He's dressed like a business man this evening—shirt and tie, slacks, dress shoes—and I sort of feel like a local downtown woman leaving my rich corporate husband for a weekend trip.

Except that I'm not.

I'm an on-call female friend—a *thot*, some might say—leaving for the airport to talk about drugs in another state, on an uncommitted lover's behalf. How pitiful is that?

So I don't wave back to Mercee. I just turn and face forward, my Prada bag on my lap, and I try to convince myself that I'm still doing the right thing. I'm helping an old friend. I know this old friend is the love of my life but I have to play my part until he knows it too.

The cab makes it halfway down Walnut Street, about to make the left turn onto Independence Avenue, when the car in front of us suddenly stops. My driver slams on his breaks, I lurch forward, slapping my palm against the backseat to stop my head from slamming into it.

"What the fuck?" I protest.

"This idiot in front of us just slammed on his brakes for no fucking reason," the cab driver says. "The turn signal is green."

"I know. Honk at him."

My cabbie pounds on the horn. *Honk-honk! Hooooonk!*

"Go around him," I say.

My cabbie turns his wheel and cautiously applies his foot to the gas. The car in front of us sees what we're trying to do and immediately cuts us off. We're now blocking oncoming traffic.

"Son of a bitch!" I holler.

It's a Volkswagen Passat in front us. I know somebody that drives that type of car. My rehab instructor—

Panic seizes me, as Wayne Rahim Layson steps out of the Passat. He marches over to our vehicle, his dreads swinging loosely, and knocks on my window hard.

"Get out the cab!" he orders.

My throat tightens. I can't speak. I told Wayne I couldn't make it to class today because I was sick.

"Get out the cab, Brandi!"

I shake my head no.

"Roll the window down." He makes a rolling gesture with his arm. I lower the window. Cars honk behind us, in front of us too. "What are you doing, Brandi?"

"Nothing."

"Why are you holding a plane ticket?"

I look down at my ticket. Kansas City to Detroit, round trip. The cab driver throws his door open, starts to get out. Wayne pulls out a black 9mm handgun and points it in the cabbie's face. *Oh fuck! Wayne has lost his mind!*

"Get back in the car," Wayne barks at him. "This is between me and the lady." He keeps the pistol trained on the cabbie until he's back in his seat, door shut. Wayne holds the gun against his thigh, out of sight. "Are you really doing this, Brandi? You came this far, Milestone status, now you're throwing it all away?"

How the fuck did he find me?

"Driver, *go!*" I plead.

"Wait!" Wayne hollers at him. Turning back to me, he speaks softly. "Brandi ... this is where all your hard work comes into play. This moment right here. Was it all for nothing? Or are you gonna adhere to the Milestone principles that you memorized by heart? Are you gonna choose right, which is Brandi, or are you gonna choose wrong, which is Mercee?"

"This plane ticket has nothing to do with Mercee," I say. "I'm going to visit family—"

"Enough!" he screams. "No more lies, Brandi. No more bullshit. No more living your life for another man. You're worth ten times more than Mercee can ever afford to give you. I know it, and you know it too, so why are you—"

"Driver, go, please!"

"—letting him control you? Why?! You don't have to please him. You don't owe him shit! Walk away, Brandi. Get out the cab. Let him sell his drugs by himself. You're tired of being used, remember?"

I hear every word Wayne is saying and it brings fresh tears to my eyes. I have no idea how he knows I'm sitting in this cab for Mercee, but it scares me. *How does he know me this well? Why is he always there for me when I don't want him to be? Why am I crying right now?*

"I love you, Brandi, just like I love every other girl in my class," he says. "I know inner beauty when I see it. That's why I push you guys so hard. I want you all to unlock your—"

I roll my window back up, drowning him out through the glass. I wipe the tears from my eyes, as I tell the cabbie to pull off before he kills us both. The cabbie inches into the wrong lane to get around Wayne's Passat, then throttles off into traffic. He asks if I'm okay and I don't respond. I turn and look out the back window.

Wayne is standing in the middle of the street, hands on his hips, watching me drive away. His face, what I can make of it, is torn with disappointment.

Tears pour down my cheeks, ruining my makeup.

I have a lot of love for Wayne, and I respect all that he does for his girls, but I love Mercee so much more.

Chapter 7

Irving Mercee, *Cocaine Kingpin*

Hands stuffed in my pockets, I walk back into the lobby of the Wallstreet Towers, feeling damn proud of myself. My operation had a kink in it, now it's falling back into place. Nysha is giving me my job back and Brandi is on her way to Detroit to secure a new customer.

I whistle a hip-hop tune as I ride the elevator back up to my condo. Then my phone rings. I check the display, see it's Nysha calling.

"Hello?" I answer as I walk off the elevator.

"Mercee, we got a big fucking problem!" she says. "I can't have any part in this. Oh my God, this is so fucked up! I'm sorry, I can't do it!"

My brow furrows. I've never heard Nysha this hysterical. "Can't do what?" I ask, as I unlock my way into my condo.

"I can't give you your job back."

I pause, then slowly close my door behind me. "Why not?"

"You're being investigated."

"Where'd you get that from? Have you been talking to Eric again? I told you to stop listening to—"

"It wasn't Eric, Mercee. The owner of B.N.I., Abe Gholson, told me this out of his own damn mouth. He said detectives want to talk to *me*. They wanna know why I fired you, even why I hired you. Somehow they know or suspect that we met before I got you a job there."

Not good. Not good at all.

I need a drink. I pour myself a glass of apple Crown and take a swig. The sweetness soothes me.

"Mercee, are you still there?"

"I'm here."

"What are we gonna do?!"

"First, I need you to calm down."

"How am I supposed to calm down?! My whole life is about to fall apart—"

"Nothing is about to fall apart, Nysha. Stop it. We just have to use our heads."

"I don't wanna go to prison, Mercee."

"And you won't," I state. "How soon can you make it downtown?"

"Downtown? What's downtown?"

"My condo."

"Your what? I thought you lived in Dunbar Gardens, those low-income apartments that you listed on your application ..." She pauses. "What else haven't you told me, Mercee?"

"Just come. We'll talk. Wallstreet Towers, 11th & Walnut."

I hang up on her, then lean against my counter and try to figure out where I went wrong to get the heat back on me. *What precaution did you overlook, Mercee?* I ponder. Coming up blank, I pick up my drink and finish it off in one swallow.

***

I hold the door open for Nysha as she walks in. She hands me my Rolex I left at her house and I strap it on, then she looks around my secret condo. A vein in her neck bulges.

"You're a liar," she says. "Lying and selling drugs—is that the only thing you're good at? Or should I say bad at?"

I offer her a drink and she declines. We sit at my large kitchen table and I pour myself another apple Crown, as she explains to me the gist of her conversation with Abe Gholson. According to her, detectives had scheduled a meeting with him, but he wanted to speak to her first. He wanted to know who I was, if she thought I was capable of outsmarting B.N.I.'s database. She told him nothing but what was in her termination report on me, that she fired me for absences. She gave him nothing else.

"You're meeting with the detectives is gonna be a lot worse," I warn her. "Their questions are gonna be tougher. They're gonna do their best to catch you in a lie."

"I don't have to talk to them."

"But you *want* to talk to them," I say.

"Why?"

"Because if you don't, they're gonna dig and dig and dig until they get something on you. So you need to give them something that leads them away from you. Tell them what you told Abe, nothing more. That should be enough. And stick to your guns."

"Should I contact them first?"

"No. Let them come to you. They know how to find you."

She plants her elbows on the table, slapping her palms against her forehead. She lets out a big sigh. I slide my glass across the table toward her. She looks at the alcohol suspiciously, then she picks it up and tastes it.

"How can you be so calm?" she asks me.

"Because we're a step ahead of them," I say. "We know they're on to us."

"That's a good thing to you?"

"To know is always a good thing. Now we know how to move."

"We can't move at all, Mercee. We have to *stop*."

I shake my head no. "I told you already. I have an obligation to my connect. We have to finish this load. It's already on its way to the B.N.I. warehouses. There's no stopping it."

"I'm not giving you your job back, Mercee. I can't."

"I know you can't. That would be stupid. But think about it: what do I need my job back for? I had the system set up how I wanted it before you fired me. And you fine-tuned my sloppy mistakes. All we have to do is sit back and let it flow."

"But systems fuck up. You know how it is at B.N.I. Packages get sorted wrong all the time. You need someone there to make sure yours is in its right zone. And what about random screening? What if one of your packages gets picked?"

"All that little stuff, you can handle. Can't you?"

Her mouth sets in a hard line. I pissed her off even more. I just asked her to move millions of dollars of cocaine for me, by herself. I did my best to make it sound like a piece of cake, but nothing about trafficking drugs is easy. Even with the world's best tech and most efficient carrier services, there's still a lot of stress involved, a lot of paranoia and loss of sleep.

It's a huge burden that a good girl like her doesn't deserve. But I have no choice.

"I need you to do this for me," I say. "I'm not asking you to risk your freedom to protect every package. I'm not asking you to carry a gun to work. But if you can press a button and delete an order to make a problem go away, then I'm asking you to press that button. That's it."

She pins me with her eyes. Then she picks up the glass in front of her, tilts it back and forth, a pinch of brown swaying to and fro. "Can you fill this back up, please?"

I bring the bottle to the table, filling hers and filling another for myself. We talk about ways to avoid any screw-ups at the warehouse, like making sure everybody involved—from the supplier in Mexico to the dealers in the U.S.—runs packaging with the highest box strength to prevent accidental tears and rips during transit. Heavy-duty, double-walled boxes only. She tells me to warn my people about stamping special markings on our packages, like the word "fragile," because some employees—the troublemakers—give these packages a beating on purpose.

I offer to pay Nysha double her salary for helping me, but she shakes her head no. "I'm not doing it for the money," she says. "I'm doing it because I love you. And because we're only doing it for another few months. I think I can handle that..." Before long, the alcohol warms her up and she confesses to me that when she was a teenager she had a crush on a guy in high school who sold drugs. She went out of her way to prove to him that she was a rebel too, by constantly cursing out school security whenever he was watching. I let out a laugh through my nose. *I love this silly girl*, I say to myself. When she tries to show me that she can fit a pencil eraser and a Skittle inside her belly button, I take her glass away and tell her she's had enough.

"You need to lay down," I say. "You can't drive home until you sober up."

"If you don't have a Skittle, I can do it with an M&M."

"I don't have either one, Nysha. Stand up. Come with me."

I lead her to my room with my hand around her waist. She sees my bed, with its carved wood headboard and motion-sensor lights that illuminate the floor on either side, and her eyes pop wide.

"Baller," she slurs. "Shot caller ..."

I lay her down, take off her shoes and pull the covers over her. She turns on her side, her eyes growing heavy. Then she sees the picture of Lucille on my nightstand.

"That's her?" she asks.

"Yep, that's her. Go to sleep."

"She's pretty. She ain't Nysha-pretty, but she's pretty."

I smile. "Go to sleep."

She closes her eyes, and in a matter of minutes she's out. I watch her sleep for a moment, wishing I had kept her sober long enough to arouse her, satisfy her, play flappy-tongue between her thighs and stroke her feverishly until both of our natures explode. She's only had sex with Mercee the fork lift driver, not Mercee *The Boss*.

I turn when I hear a knock on my front door. Every other day one of the maintenance guys are here, giving residents advance notice on temporary power outages, or asking to sign ordinance waivers, introduce new maintenance policies, and sometimes just to talk. I rarely have time for any of it.

I open the door, surprised to see Brandi Nieman. She has tears in her eyes.

"What are you doing here?" I ask, irritated. I look at my Rolex. "Don't tell me you missed your flight."

"I did miss it," she says.

"How, Brandi? You left here with plenty of time to spare."

"I was sitting by myself in the terminal, thinking about us. I'm not comfortable doing this without you. We always took our trips together, Mercee. We had each other's back. I feel like you don't have my back this time." A tear traces down her cheek.

"I do have your back. I just got a lot to juggle and I can't be everywhere at one time. Brandi, you should've called me before you left the airport. This is bullshit. I got people in Detroit waiting to pick you up from DTW right now. What am I gonna say to them when you don't show, huh? How am I supposed to—"

I stop when I see her mouth drop open. She's looking over my shoulder in horror. I turn and look. Nysha is walking clumsily across my living room. She finds the bathroom door, struggles with the knob, then disappears inside.

"Who the fuck was that!" Brandi screams. She tries to push her way into my condo. I push back.

"Brandi, no," I say.

"Let me in! Who is that bitch!"

"None of your fucking business!"

She backs up, panting like she's out of breath. She stares at me like she has no idea who I am. Then she storms off down the hall.

I go after her, grabbing her arm before she reaches the elevator. "Hold up, Brandi."

She whirls around, smacking me hard across the face. "None of my business? You want me to travel state to state for you, risking my life and my freedom, and a ho inside yo condo is none of my business?"

I don't know what to say to her.

"Wayne was right. You are a trespasser. You're the worst kind."

"Who is Wayne?"

"My rehab instructor, my mentor, somebody that believes in me and my growth as a woman. Somebody that doesn't make you feel good just to rip your heart out later. Do you really think I'm gonna do your shitwork for you while you sit here and hump on a bunch of bitches in your fancy condo?"

"It's not like that, Brandi. You know I'm not the ho type."

"So that bitch means something to you?"

I don't reply.

She chokes out a cry, holds back her tears as she backs away from me. "I don't believe this. I don't believe *you*. I don't believe myself for being so stupid."

"Brandi, where are you going?"

"To class, where I should've already been. I'm a Milestone girl. We don't take no shit from trespassers."

"We need to talk, air things out. After your class, call me. We can reschedule the Detroit trip for another day."

She flips me the bird as the elevator doors close.

I squeeze my eyes shut, pinching the bridge of my nose. *Goddamn, Mercee.* If it's not one thing, it's another.

Then I turn and see Nysha standing in the hallway in her work shirt and panties.

Fuck.

Chapter 8

Wayne Layson, *Rehab Instructor*

"Our Milestone girl, Brandi Nieman, was supposed to open the class today ... but regrettably she couldn't make it," I say to the room full of women. "She called in sick. So I'll be opening up for us this time, if you ladies don't mind."

"Go 'head, speak, brother," Cynthia DuLord calls out from the second row. A chorus of cheers and whistles spreads through the room, then they all receive me with a warm round of applause.

But I notice that one of my girls isn't clapping. Yee'sha Clark, who's sitting directly behind Cynthia, is looking down at her smartphone studiously. Reading assignments, I hope.

"One of our newest members," I say aloud, "completed her first worksheet on self-reliance with an eighty-five percent. Yee'sha Clark. Let's give her a hand, ladies."

The mention of her name jolts her. Yee'sha stuffs her phone in her pocket, as the class claps loudly for her.

"Would you like to stand up and let your peers know what you've learned so far?" I ask.

She pouts her lips, thinking about it. "Mmmm, no."

I smile, as a few other girls share a giggle. "Don't be shy," I say. "Everybody who doesn't already know, Yee'sha is nineteen years old, the youngest girl in our class. I think it says a lot about her character and maturity, being that she's so young and hasn't missed a day of class yet. Please welcome her to the podium with all the love you have."

More applause.

With a labored sigh, Yee'sha stands and scoots past the girls in her row and drags herself up to the front of the room. She crosses her arms, then looks at me as if she's waiting for me to tell her what to say.

I point to the class. *Address them, not me.*

She huffs. "Um ... I've learned a lot about depending on myself instead of depending on a pimp to make me feel special or to take care of me financially. When you depend on other people to make you happy, you open yourself up to ..." Her forehead scrunches. She looks at me for the answer.

"Trespassing," I say.

"Yeah, trespassing. It's like mind control, I guess. In the beginning of the self-reliance worksheet it asks you if you believe in mind control. That's one thing I've learned so far. Mind control is real. If you're not in control of your mind, that means somebody else is. Because the brain can't operate without direction or stimulus."

I nod in agreement.

Sometimes I tend to compare a lot of the girls with each other. Not on purpose. It just happens. Watching Yee'sha now, speaking as if she's suffering from boredom, reminds me of Brandi Nieman when she first started my class. Brandi had an air of arrogance about her. She felt like she was better than the other addicts in the class because her trespasser was a kingpin, a young multi-millionaire. She drove Ferraris and Bentleys and Lamborghinis and traveled all over the world before she was of legal age. I think that Yee'sha's arrogance comes from her having college credits. A lot of the other girls never finished high school. Some of them can't even read.

It was hell trying to humble Brandi. And I'm sure it'll be the same way with Yee'sha. I failed to re-purpose Brandi. I don't plan to fail Yee'sha.

I stand back up and give Yee'sha a hug, thanking her for sharing her thoughts with the class. Then I take over again, using this time to harp on the importance of my two favorite topics—leadership and habit-forming—and also of knowing the difference between physical survival and psychological survival. I lay eyes on Cynthia and Yee'sha, as they both shared the same pimp, Lee Thomas Mayfield. He tortured them both with all the devices of a classic trespasser—demeaning language, random physical abuse, abandonment, death threats, acting as the sole source of their validation. Even though Lee Thomas Mayfield is now dead (from circumstances that me and Yee'sha agreed to take to the grave), there is still room for another trespasser to come in and make a home. Cynthia and Yee'sha share a void, as Lee Thomas Mayfield's death is still fresh in their minds. My job is to fill that void with love.

"We're taught in school that physical survival is number one," I say to everyone, holding my forefinger up high. Then I slowly uncurl my middle finger. "Number two, they say, is psychological survival. But to put them in numerical order is to suggest that one comes after the other. In actuality, they go hand in hand. Can't have one without the other. Can't have rhythm without the blues."

My class laughs at my poor analogy.

"We know that physical survival is feeding yourself. Food, water, shelter. It's also self-defense. If somebody tries to kill you, you do what? You fight back. You kick, you punch, you might even pick up a rock—"

"Or a frying pan!" one girl shouts vehemently, followed by laughter.

"Or a Taurus .380!" another yells.

"But what do you use to defend yourself against psychological attacks?" I ask.

The room falls silent.

"I'll name off a few weapons you can use against psychological warfare. You can use the sword of self-respect, or the machine gun of positive principles, or the integrity guillotine. I'll show all of you how to use these weapons and many-many more. Before you finish this class, you ladies are gonna be strapped to the tee. Certified, take-no-shit Rambo-ettes."

My train of thought falters off when I see a woman walk through the door at the other end of the room. The whole class turns to look.

Brandi Nieman strolls in, wearing a pair of dark sunglasses. I can see traces of tears that have streaked down her cheeks. She sits in the very back row, as if a Milestone girl has the ability to go unnoticed here.

"Brandi, come speak with me, please," I say.

She stands and walks to the front of the class, all eyes on her. I tell Cynthia to take over for a moment while me and Brandi talk in private.

I close my office door and lock it.

"Brandi ..." I say softly, removing her sunglasses for her. She puts her head down. I lift her chin and she looks me in the eyes. "... You did it."

I smile. She bursts into tears and I wrap my arms around her, holding her as close and tight as I can. I was certain I had lost her to her trespasser. But she came back.

"He doesn't love me!" she cries. "Mercee doesn't love me!"

"Shhhh. It's okay."

"He just wanted to use me. He never loved me. It's always somebody else that he treats better than me."

"Did he hurt you?"

"No. He just grabbed my arm, tried to stop me from getting on the elevator. But he didn't even really try that hard. It's like he wanted me to leave."

I hold her face in my hands and kiss her on the lips, then plant my forehead against hers. "Brandi, don't let him make you think that you aren't wanted. You *are* wanted. You are loved. You are a great woman. You are a cherished human being."

She says, "As soon as he stuck me in that taxi, he had another girl on the way to his condo. He didn't even wait five minutes before calling another—"

"Brandi, I don't care. What matters is you didn't get on that plane. You didn't make that trip for him. You did it, Brandi!" I squeeze her face. "You fucking did it!"

She closes her eyes and takes a deep breath. When she opens them, she looks into my eyes with all the vulnerability of a child at her best friend's funeral. I embrace her in a hug again, reassuring her.

"Will you be able to sit through class with us?" I ask her.

"I'm here," she states.

"You don't have to participate if you don't want to."

"Okay." She takes a breath. "Can I put my glasses back on? I don't want the rest of the class to see a Milestone girl this messed up."

"Go right ahead."

She slips her shades on and I take her around the shoulder, leading her back to the group. I notice that the class's attention is focused on the back of the room, where Cynthia is speaking with someone.

A visitor.

A man.

"You can't come in here," Cynthia says to him.

"I'm looking for Brandi," the visitor says.

"She's not here."

The visitor steps around Cynthia, laying eyes on Brandi—and I lay eyes on him.

It's Irving Mercee!

"Brandi, c'mere," he says. "We need to talk."

Brandi looks at me in horror. "What do I do?"

I grab her hand, interlocking our fingers. "Don't be afraid," I say. "I'm here with you. We're all here with you. But you have to face him on your own."

"I didn't tell him to come here."

"I know. But only you have the power to send him on his way."

Cynthia stands in front of Mercee again. "You're not allowed in here. No trespassers allowed. Get the fuck out!"

"Cynthia, this isn't your battle," I say. "Get away from him."

"Please chill," Mercee says to her. "I'm just here to talk to my lady. Then I'll leave."

I feel Brandi's fingers loosen, as if she wants to let go of my hand. Mercee's "my lady" comment had an affect on her. I grip her hand tighter.

"Be strong," I hiss.

Cynthia pushes her chest against Mercee. "You're leaving now, goddammit! Ain't nobody scared of you here. Your tough shit doesn't fly—"

Mercee shoves her away with his forearm, takes a step toward Brandi—and then something remarkable happens. Every girl in the class stands to their feet (not all at once, but still all), blocking Mercee from passing. Euphoria blasts through my body. I've never seen this before. My girls are standing in solidarity, facing a trespasser head-on!

Mercee hollers over the heads in the crowd, "Brandi, don't let these people tell you what you need to do! You know where you belong. We're a team. These muthafuckas in here are crazy. You're not one of them. C'mon, let's get out of here."

Brandi lets my hand go. I snatch her by the wrist.

"Don't give in," I snap at her.

"I'm just going to talk to him."

"Talk?" I ask. "Or are you going to demand to be heard?"

"I'm going to demand to be heard."

I let her wrist go, and she slips through the crowd and walks right up to Mercee. He tries to usher her outside but she jerks away.

I smile.

"Brandi, I don't wanna talk in front of these—"

She cuts him off. "Listen to me, Mercee. I'm not the same person that's gonna sit back and be treated—"

"Let's not do this here," he says.

But Brandi fires right back. "If you interrupt me one more time, you might as well turn around and walk back out that door. Don't interrupt me, Mercee."

The class claps for her. I clap too.

"I'm not gonna let you treat me any kind of way anymore," she continues. "I will never again settle for number two. I know what I'm worth. I know I'm priceless, in mind and in body. And since your value of me doesn't come close to my estimates, I have to say *no deal*. I'm done, Mercee. Get out of here."

"Is that what you think?" he says. "You think I'm tryna play you? You think that girl you saw in my condo is number one?"

"Who was she?"

I cringe. *Bad question, Brandi.* She shouldn't be worried about who the girl was. The fact that there is a girl, period, should be enough to drop him. I wish I could speak for Brandi. I wish I could jump inside her body and rattle her brain, breaking loose all of her emotional ties to him.

"She's a project," Mercee tells her. "That's all I can say in here, in front of these people. That girl means nothing to me. She don't mean shit. If you'll let me explain myself outside, in private, you'll understand."

"You're hurting me again, Mercee."

"Again?"

"Yes, again! First it was random hos here and there. Then you left me completely for Lucille."

"Brandi, we were kids back then. You can't hold that against me. That's like me holding against you all the shit you put me through. Did you forget how much we lost behind your addiction?"

Guilt. I hope Brandi sees it. This is elementary trespasser manipulation. I speak about this during almost every class.

"Who do you think drove me to my addiction? You did, Mercee!" she shouts, and her passion gives me goosebumps. "I turned to crack-cocaine because I couldn't turn to you anymore."

"Brandi, we can go back and forth all day playing the blame game, but that's not what I wanna do. I thought we were past this. I thought we were starting fresh."

"We were, until I showed up at your condo tonight and you had another woman there. You can go start fresh with her."

We all clap for her again. And someone even finger-whistles—a sharp, clear sound of triumph.

Mercee looks around the crowd of women, sees that he's outnumbered. Then he finds me. Our eyes lock for a moment, and I flash a winning smile—*Your mind games don't work here, Mercee.* He turns back to Brandi, then tilts his head toward her and whispers in her ear.

I wish I could hear what he's saying to her. My deluxe headphones are right down the hall, in my office, but if I run to go slap them on, I could miss something important.

A moment later Mercee leans away from her and says softly, "Make a choice." Then he turns and walks away, walks right out of the main entrance without looking back.

Brandi wipes tears from her eyes. Then she gazes at all of us, unsure of herself. Taking a deep breath, she starts toward me—and along the way she's celebrated with pats on the back, more whistles and cheers—"Go, Brandi!" "You the shit, girl!"—until me and her are face to face.

I smile. A tear falls from my eye.

"I knew you would make me proud," I say. "I knew you deserved the Milestone—"

She cuts me off. "I have to go."

My chest tightens. "Go? No, Brandi. Absolutely not."

"I'm sorry, Wayne."

"What did he say to you?"

Tears start pouring down her cheeks. She repeats herself. "I have to go."

"You're quitting?"

"No, I'm not quitting. I know what happens when I quit. You send me to jail." She stares deep into my eyes, unblinking. "I'm going to finish your program, Wayne. I am. I will. Just not today."

She turns on her heels and walks away from me, picking up her pace as she passes through the center aisle of chairs, where her peers are standing on either side of her, watching her go, sad and bewildered by her decision to follow her trespasser.

"What did he say to you?" I call out. But Brandi keeps walking, shrugging her purse strap on her shoulder. So I scream, "What the fuck did he say to you, Brandi!"

Then she's gone.

Chapter 9

Nysha Hawk, *Manager*

Halfway into mile three, I start to feel the burn in my thighs. My breathing is ragged, sweat drenches the neckline of my sports bra, and I'm low on water.

But I keep my legs moving. I have to, in order to keep my mind off the reminder that what I've done for Mercee— and what I'm *still* doing—could land me in federal prison for a very long time.

Jogging along the Waldo-area sidewalks is my escape. I love the wind against my flushed cheeks, the respectful eye contact of fellow joggers as we pass each other, even the slight fear of car danger as I pace through crosswalks. Cardio always takes me away from my problems.

Momentarily.

Besides the mess that Mercee stuck me with at work, there's another thought that's bothering me this morning. I remember going to Mercee's condo and telling him about my talk with my boss, Abe Gholson. I remember drinking way too much, blacking out, then awaking in his bed. I had trouble walking to his bathroom, nearly falling over with each step. I vomited in his toilet, rinsed my mouth. I looked over, eyeing a gold Versace bath towel hanging on the towel rack. I remember thinking that it seemed too nice for me to use, so I dried my mouth with toilet paper. When I came out of the bathroom, I saw his front door wide open.

I started to close it, but I heard him arguing with a woman.

I stepped into the hallway, saw him, saw her. My memory tells me she was brown-skinned, and pretty. Long beautiful hair, big earrings, sexy skintight dress—she was the kind of woman I'd expect a drug kingpin to date. I remember telling myself that I needed to mind my own business—*and your head is pounding, girl, lay your ass back down*—then wandering back to his bed.

The next morning I asked Mercee about the girl in the hallway. He told me there was no girl, that I had been drunk. I had dreamed it all.

But how did I remember everything else about the night?

Did Mercee lie to me?

Now, as I force my legs to power through mile five, I tell myself that if the girl was real, then it could've been a neighbor he was arguing with. Or maybe it wasn't an argument—it could've been friendly chatter.

Or he could have been telling the truth—there never was any girl.

I stop at the corner of 72nd Street, bending over to catch my breath. I down the rest of my water, then walk over to the gas station, where I use my charge card for a Slurpee.

"You're gonna get caught with that cocaine," I hear the clerk say to me, as he places my receipt in my palm.

My heart stops. "Excuse me?" I say.

"I said don't get caught in the rain."

I look outside and see dark clouds moving in from the west. I breathe a sigh of relief. *He was just talking about the coming storm, Nysha. Chill out. You're being paranoid for nothing.*

I walk to my car, sipping my Slurpee. Thunder rumbles across the sky as I climb in my Mustang, starting it up. Light rain patters my windshield, then in no time it's hammering down and I can barely see the road, even with my wipers at full blast. I make it to my street and turn in my driveway. Grabbing my umbrella from the backseat, I throw my door open and pop open my umbrella, then I make a run for it, chin to my chest, the sideways rain tagging my yoga pants from the waist down.

I jump on my porch and—

"Ms. Hawk, how are you?"

I scream.

"It's okay," one of the two men says, showing me a police badge. "We're detectives. My name is Detective Frisk. This is my partner, Detective Copeland."

I look at both men. One is brown-skinned, dressed in a suit and tie, his umbrella collapsed and tucked under his arm; the other is a darker shade of brown, wearing a navy blue KCPD pullover glistening with rain water, its hood pulled up. I didn't see either of them when I turned in my driveway. They had been standing in the nook of my entryway, against the siding, out of sight.

Detectives.

At my door.

My heartrate intensifies.

Thunder booms behind me and I flinch, dropping my phone. It lands on the stoop, face up. The screen automatically alights, displaying my screen saver—me and Mercee cheek to cheek, wearing our aviator headsets around our necks. Specks of rain starts to blur the screen.

"I got it," says Copeland, as he bends over to pick it up.

"No." I squat down, snatch my phone. Copeland looks at me strangely. "Who sent you here?" I ask.

"We had a talk with your boss, Abe Gholson," says Detective Frisk. "He said you might be able to help us with our investigation."

"He sent you guys to my house?"

The detectives glance at one another. Frisk says, "No, he didn't tell us to come here. We got your address from motor vehicle records, came here in hopes that—"

"Do you have a warrant?"

"No, we don't," Frisk says. "You're not in any trouble. We just wanted to talk to you about one of your employees. Irving Mercee. Would you like us to come back at another time?"

Mercee told me they'd come. He told me not to avoid them or they'd be suspicious.

"Uh ... I guess you guys can come in if you'd like," I say.

I show them inside. Frisk hangs his suit jacket on the back of my front door. Copeland pulls his jacket off too, and hooks it. They offer to wipe up the water they tracked in.

"I'll get it later," I say. "Drinks? Water? Coffee?"

They both ask for coffee. I give them their cups, along with a glass saucer, and we sit in my living room.

"If you need time to change out of those wet clothes, we'll wait," says Copeland. "We don't want to inconvenience you."

"I'm already inconvenienced," I say.

Frisk clears his throat. "Ms. Hawk, we only have a few simple questions and then we'll be out of your hair." He sips his coffee. His face turns sour. "Strong, he says. Just how I like it. Thank you."

"You're welcome."

"So you're familiar with Mr. Irving Mercee?"

"I am."

"How familiar?" Copeland asks.

"He worked in my section of the warehouse," I say. "I knew him just as well as I knew a hundred other employees in my section."

Frisk says, "You hired him, right?"

"Yes."

"Did you know he was a felon?"

"I knew he had a criminal background. Lots of guys and girls who drive forklifts have backgrounds. What did he do this time?"

"We'll get to that," Copeland says.

Frisk lays a folder on my coffee table, opens it up. As he peeks at each page inside, he says, "We found these notes that Mercee left behind in prison. If you take a look at him, you'll see that he targeted your company, and he targeted you specifically."

"What do you mean he targeted me?"

"Take a look."

Frisk hands me the notes and I look at them, narrowing my eyes when the type turns small. I see my name over and over again, in printed material off of the company website, and even in Mercee's own handwriting. If these notes are real, then that means Mercee knew who I was before we met at that supermarket last year. I remember him bumping into my cart—on accident, I had thought—and apologizing and introducing himself, as if he had no idea who I was.

I feel a headache coming on.

Mercee, you fucking liar.

"Did he highlight my name, or did you guys?" I ask.

"He did," says Frisk. "This is all his handiwork. We haven't tampered with it at all."

"Did he have any contact with you before he applied for a job at B.N.I.?" asks Detective Copeland.

I hesitate, as I stare at a green checkmark that Mercee placed next to my B.N.I. company photo. I also see what looks like the words "pretty" and "best option" scrawled on the page. I was smiling in the pic, my hair short and feathered.

He referred to me as an "option."

"Any contact at all," Copeland presses. "He's a slick mofo, Nysha. He uses people to get his way. That's his M.O. If there's something you can tell us, then please do."

I flip to another page, where reports on B.N.I.'s stocks are listed. "No, he didn't contact me prior to his interview at Black Nile," I lie.

"Are you sure?" Copeland asks.

"Positive."

The detectives tell me that Mercee is under investigation for cocaine distribution. They believe he's moving or has moved cocaine through B.N.I. and they want my take on it. I tell them what I told Abe: "If I would have caught him doing anything illegal, I would've reported it," I say. I tell them I fired Mercee for attendance issues, and they pretend as if they didn't already know.

"If he contacts you from this point forward, or you remember something about his activities that might suddenly seem helpful to our investigation, then don't hesitate to give us a call." Frisk hands me his business card. "Thanks for your time, Ms. Hawk."

I walk them to the door. As Copeland slips on his pullover, he asks me, "Are you single?"

But his partner, Frisk, pulls him out into the rain before I can answer. I shut the door and lock it.

I take out my phone, toggling through its interface until I view the home screen settings. I tap the screensaver tab and the photo of me and Mercee with our aviator headsets appears.

I should've done this a long time ago, I say to myself.

Then I tap delete, removing the evidence of our relationship.

Chapter 10

Michael Frisk, *Detective*

"I can't believe you asked her that," I say to Copeland, as I reverse out of Ms. Hawk's driveway. "What the hell were you thinking, asking that woman if she's single?"

"I had my reasons," he replies smartly.

"Please share. Because if they had anything to do with sex, then I'm telling your baby's mother."

He chuckles.

"I'm serious!" I bark. "We don't need your horny little hormones interfering with this investigation this time. I saw how you were looking at C.O. Sarah Hamilton when we were in Greenville. Now you come out here and hit on a person of interest. What the hell, Copeland? Get yourself together. Grow up."

I look out my window and see Nysha peeking out of the front room curtains, as I shift down into gear. I wave. She shuts the curtains.

I drive off, clicking on my windshield wipers.

"I think you scared her," I say.

Copeland lights a blunt, and I push the buttons on my door panel to lower all four windows. He blows smoke out in a quick stream, then says, "She was scared of us before we even walked in her house."

"Probably because of the way you were ogling her."

"No, it's because she's hiding something."

"Like what?"

"Her relationship with Mercee."

I glance over at him. "What kind of relationship are you talking about?"

"He's fucking her," Copeland says. "He's giving that bitch the pipe. That's why she wouldn't give us shit."

"And how'd you come up with that?"

"When she dropped her phone, her screensaver popped up. It was her and Mercee, hugged up close to each other."

"Bullshit."

"Okay, don't believe me." He shrugs, takes another puff of his marijuana, then releases. Smoke wafts in the air, bouncing off the windshield, spreading my way.

I lower my window even more. "Are you sure it was Mercee?"

"I'm sure. When I bent over to pick up her phone, to get a better look, she hurried up and snatched it. The screen was a little blurry from the rain that sprinkled on it, but I know Mercee when I see him."

"You think she knows what he's been doing at B.N.I.? Or do you think she's just protecting her man from prosecution?"

"I don't know. She could be helping him."

"Think so? She hasn't known him that long. Why would she risk her freedom for him?"

"Women do the craziest shit when they fall in love. I knew a chick two weeks, she wanted me to move in with her. She didn't want me to work, leave, nothing. She just wanted a man indoors at all times."

"Nysha doesn't strike me as that type. If she was helping him, why would she fire him?"

"Maybe Abe told her about the investigation and she fired him to protect him."

"It's possible," I say.

"You think Knam will let us get a wiretap on her?"

I look over at Copeland again. His eyes are bloodshot now. "Not like that, he won't."

"What?" Copeland flips down the visor, inspecting his face in the mirror.

I keep my eyes on the road, focusing on the yellow divider lines—they're all I can see in this downpour. I wonder if Nysha really is helping Mercee. And if so, who else does he have wrapped around his finger?

Chapter 11

Irving Mercee, *Cocaine Kingpin*

I knock on the wide glass, trying to get Lucille's attention. She turns, but not because she hears me—she's merely moving in a circle, rocking our newborn baby in her arms.

"Bring him over here," I say.

She doesn't hear me. I knock on the glass again.

Then I happen to look down at the floor near her feet. I see water, a small stream of it, oozing from underneath our child's incubator, flowing past its wheels, edging close to Lucille's flip-flops.

I think nothing of it—until I see water creeping in from every corner of the room.

"Lucille, you might wanna come on outta there," I say with urgency, knocking harder on the glass. "They have some kind of leak. Look down, Lucille. Look down."

She still doesn't respond.

Frustrated, I spin away from the glass in search of help, or a way inside the nursery to yank Lucille and our son out of there.

But I can't.

All around me are steel bars, erect and unmoving, caging me in. I'm in a prison cell!

I turn back to the nursery's glass window—and I see the most horrific sight of my life. The water in the nursery is now over my head, and Lucille is floating underwater, her face pressed against the glass. Then, as her hair floats away from her face, I realize it isn't Lucille's face at all.

It's Nysha ... Her eyes are closed, as if she's sleeping. Her face is pale, lips icy blue.

Then her eyes pop open.

***

The nightmare jerks me awake.

"Baby, you okay?" asks Brandi.

I sit up in my seat, wiping a spittle of saliva from the corner of my mouth with the back of my hand. I unfasten my seatbelt, throwing it aside.

"The plane is about to land," Brandi warns me. "Where are you going?"

I look past her, outside her plane window. All I can see is flashes of clouds, our commercial aircraft descending through the fog rapidly. I had no idea where I was about to go. I just wanted to escape, so I could help Lucille ... or Nysha.

It was just a dream, I tell myself.

"Why didn't you wake me up?" I ask her, as I buckle up again.

"I'm never waking you up again, especially while on a plane. The last time I woke you up while we were on a plane, you smacked me."

"I apologized right after I did that."

"Yes, you did." She smiles. "I know you didn't mean it. Hell, I deserved it."

"We had a lot of dope on that plane, and that really wasn't the best time to play games."

"Mercee, I know that. I'm grown now." She kisses me on the cheek. "But I'm still not waking yo black ass up ever again. You better set an alarm."

After we land, me and Brandi wheel our carry-on luggage up the jet bridge and into the terminal. My cell phone immediately starts going crazy once I take it off airplane mode. I have a ton of missed calls and text messages.

And they're all from Nysha Hawk.

Brandi says, "It's her, isn't it?"

I show her my phone. "Every single notification is from her."

"I never blew you up like that. I don't care what I needed you for, I always said what I had to say and I'd wait for your response. That bitch has no patience or respect for your time."

I had to tell Brandi my position with Nysha. It was the only way to get her to walk out of that rehab center. I told her that Nysha is a floor manager at B.N.I., that I have to sleep with her from time to time in order to insure that all of our packages arrive and depart on schedule, untampered. I promised Brandi I'd be open and honest about everything, business and personal. I had also whispered, "... from this point on, we're taking all out-of-town trips together, just like old times." It won her over. She told her weird-ass instructor goodbye and marched out of those doors with her chin up.

I tap Nysha's contact number on my screen, then put the phone up to my ear. Nysha didn't leave any voicemails or clues in her texts as to what she's been trying to reach me about. All her messages were, "Call me now," "Where are you," "I need to talk to you now," "Mercee, where are you," and her last text was alarmingly ominous: "I'm not doing this shit anymore."

Yes, you are, I say in my head.

Nysha picks up. "Where are you, Mercee? I've been trying to call you like crazy!"

"I just landed in Detroit," I say, while looking at Brandi. She's in earshot, but she's staring at her phone as if she's not interested in my conversation.

"Detroit? You left me here to deal with this shit by myself?"

"Deal with what?"

"Detectives showed up at my house, asking questions."

"Okay, what's the problem? We talked about this."

"Yes, we talked about it, but I didn't think they would come to my goddamn house! That's not normal, is it?"

"It is normal, Nysha. They'll come to your house, your job, your momma's job, wherever they have to go to follow up on a lead. They're desperate for information."

"They must know there's something going on between us."

"They only know what you told them," I say. "What'd you tell them?"

"Nothing. I told them I hired you and I fired you. They asked if I knew you had a criminal background and I said all I knew was that you were a felon, and that didn't bother me because we hire lots of felons."

"You did your part then."

"What if they come back?"

"They won't. They followed a lead and hit a dead end. We have nothing to worry about, baby."

Brandi looks up, frowning at my use of the word "baby." I turn away from her.

"Nysha, they won't bother you anymore," I say into the phone. "They have no reason to. You told them what you know, now they have to move on. Everything is fine."

She pauses, then says, "Why didn't you tell me you were going to Detroit?"

"It was a last-minute thing. I had someone else going at first, but they missed their flight so I have to fill in. Like

I said, it was last minute. I didn't think to call you because I was so focused on making sure this meeting happened today. I took a red-eye flight. I had to sleep on the plane."

"Is Zaki with you?" she asks.

"No."

"You're by yourself?"

"Yes," I lie.

"When are you coming back?"

"Tomorrow."

She breathes into the phone. "There's something else I need to tell you," she says nervously. "The owner, Abe Gholson, sent me an email about an hour ago saying he needs to talk to me this afternoon. I don't know, Mercee, this might not be good. This is the second time this month. He might be letting me go, too."

"Don't think like that. You haven't did anything to get fired."

"Yes, I have."

"Nothing that he knows about," I say. "Think positive."

"I'm trying to."

"Try harder."

I tell her I'll call her after my business is finished here in Detroit, before I board my flight back to Kansas City, then I hang up.

Brandi was waiting for my call to end. "She's gonna crack," she says. "Most women can't hold up to this type of pressure. Nysha is gonna sing like a bird the first chance she gets."

"No, she's not," I say back. "If she was, she would've told on me as soon as she found those drugs in the warehouse."

"What does Zaki think about her?"

"The same thing he thinks about you. He doesn't like her."

"But he was okay with her knowing about the operation?"

Zaki doesn't know yet. I haven't told him that Nysha unboxed some of our cocaine and drug money and that I had to come clean, telling her that we're moving millions worth of illegal narcotics in and out of B.N.I. He'd want to kill her, no question in my mind. That's his answer to everything—murder, torture, murder, murder, torture. So I'm holding off on telling him as long as I can.

"Let's just get our rental and go make this deal happen," I say to Brandi, stuffing my phone in my pocket.

I tug my carry-on bag behind me, wheeling it through the terminal quickly, forcing Brandi to keep up.

Chapter 12

Nysha Hawk, *Manager*

I knock on Abe's office door.

"Come in," he says from the other side.

I open it, walking in slowly. I'm facing him as my fingers push the door shut behind me. While twirling a ballpoint pen through each finger of his right hand, he stares at me from the top of my head down to the rubber toe of my work boots, in a way that suggests he's deciding what to do with me.

My heart races as I take a seat.

"Back already?" he says, as if I came here on my own free will.

"I got your email," I say.

"Do you have any idea why I requested to see you again?"

"No."

"I'm sure you have a clue."

I clear my throat. "Is it about Mercee?"

He drops his pen in a cup with several other writing utensils. "Correct."

I flinch as he springs to his feet. He buttons his suit jacket and walks over to the only window in his office, a wall-to-wall window with a bird's-eye view of the eastern section of the warehouse.

"You've been a busy girl," he says to me, as he gazes out at all of his hourly workers below. "Busy-busy, Ms. Hawk. You've always been a productive girl, so I shouldn't be surprised."

I've never felt fear like this in my life.

"Haven't you?" he asks.

"I don't know what you mean," I say with tremors in my voice.

He turns and looks at me, confusion creasing his brow. "One of my top floor managers doesn't know the meaning of busy?"

"I know what the word means but—"

"You fired somebody recently."

I frown. "You already knew I fired Mercee."

"I'm not talking about Mercee."

"But you said this meeting was about Mercee."

"It is."

With my elbows resting on the arm rests of my chair, I turn my palms up. "I'm confused," I say.

"Eric Alden?"

"Oh," I say, remembering. "Eric. Yes, I did fire Eric. It's just been so much going on lately, I forgot."

"Why'd you fire him?"

"I caught him selling weed."

"And you don't see how this relates to Mercee?"

It dawns on me suddenly: *Abe thinks Eric works for Mercee.*

"Eh?" Abe says, smiling. "You're figuring it out. But I thought you already knew. I thought that's why you fired him."

"No, I didn't think Eric's situation had anything to do with Mercee's. I fired Eric because I caught him selling weed in the break room. That's not tolerated here at B.N.I. and it really pissed me off. I apologize for not going through all the proper HR procedures, but I did write down why I fired him in his report."

Abe walks toward me, then around the back of my chair—my eyes follow his circle—and he sits in front of me, on the edge of his desk. "You did the right thing," he says. "Nicholas Rolfe happened to bring it to my attention that somebody was recently fired for selling drugs. I don't think it's a coincidence that Mercee and Eric both worked in your zone."

My nerves are strung tight. I'm afraid to move.

"And I don't think it's a coincidence that you fired them both," he continues. "You got rid of two bad guys.

Busy, busy girl, always got your eye on things. Nothing gets past you. And I wanna thank you."

I relax a little. I tell him, "I don't deserve thanks, Abe. I was just doing my job."

"Let me take you to lunch."

Is he asking me out again? I say to myself in disbelief.

"May I?" he presses.

"I wasn't going to take a lunch today," I say. "I have way too much work to do."

"Nonsense." He stands up, holds his hand out to take mine.

"Right now?" I ask.

"Yes, now."

"It's still another hour till lunch."

"I'm the boss. Lunch is when I say it is."

I reluctantly give my hand to him and he helps me up. We walk together out of his office, his hand resting on the small of my back. As we pass through the warehouse, eyes of my co-workers are on me and him, and I get the self-conscious notion that they all know we used to date, even though our past relationship was top secret (as far as I know). He holds the door open to the B.N.I. cafeteria. When we enter, the place is vacant, save for a few prep cooks.

"What do you want?" he asks.

I look across the buffet line. All the metal trays are empty. "There's nothing to pick from," I say with a laugh.

"Nysha, you've worked here long enough to know the menu by heart. Tell me what you want. I'll have them slap it together right away."

I have no appetite—I'm still a smidge nervous, overly worried about being discovered as Mercee's co-conspirator—but I name a dish off the top of my head anyway.

"Lasagna," I say. It's a meal Mercee always wants me to cook.

"Lasagna it is," Abe says. "And I think I'll have the same."

He summons a cook and tells them our order, then we have a seat in a couple slat-back chairs at a lone, metal table in a sea of other unoccupied tables. I've never been in here without it being jam-packed, waiting in long, slow lines, noisy banter all at once all around you, then fighting for a good seat at a clean table. This quietness in this big cafeteria is a first for me.

I don't like it.

"You wanna know something that I found out about Mercee?" Abe whispers, leaning over the table like a kid who can't hold in a secret.

I merely blink, because my anxiety is revving up again, holding me completely still.

"He doesn't live in Dunbar Gardens. It was a dummy address."

"How do you know?" I ask.

"Because I checked it out. I physically went there and knocked on the door. Nobody answered. I went and introduced myself to the property manager and found out that Mercee is in fact renting the space, paying on time every month and everything, but he doesn't *live* there. So I shook the property manager's hand, paid him to make me a personal key to Mercee's apartment and I went inside."

"You what? Abe, are you crazy? That's the police's job. You're the president of a billion-dollar company. You're not supposed to do crazy stuff like that."

"I didn't get where I am today by being perfectly sane. You have to be a little nuts to reach a level of my status. Besides, the police are slow. If corporation owners like myself ran the law, there would be no crime. Executives know how to get shit done ahead of schedule."

I shake my head disapprovingly.

"But guess what I found inside?" he said.

"What?"

He smiles. "Nothing ... ab-so-fucking-lutely nothing. Zilch. This fucker Mercee really is a different type of criminal. The only thing in there was a few pieces of mock furniture and brown carpet, the cleanest I've ever seen. He probably never spent one night in that apartment. I can't believe that guy."

Abe is taking this insight into his former employee rather well, it seems. When I found out about the real Irving Mercee, I was devastated. I still am.

"The police came and talked to me," I say. "They came to my house. They were there after I came home from jogging."

Abe scowls. "I told those muthafuckas to contact me about setting up a meeting with you. I was gonna let you speak to them at your own leisure, whenever you had time. Now they've fucking pissed me off."

"When are they gonna stop investigating this?"

"I don't know, Nysha. Cases involving lots of drugs are federal and can stretch on for years. But I'm here today to tell you that that's not gonna happen this time. The KCPD can go fuck themselves if they think I'm gonna let that fly. I know some important people in the department, I'm friends with the mayor and most other politicians in Missouri that matter, so you can rest assured that those detectives won't be harassing my beautiful Nysha ever again. I'ma make sure of that."

I give a faint smile. I'm beginning to think Abe can be an ally, as long as he never finds out my role in Mercee's plan. *Six more months*, I remind myself. *Then Mercee will be finished and things will get back to normal.*

"I have my own investigative team working on Mercee," Abe says. "I was skeptical at first, but now I believe without a doubt that he was pushing drugs through my company— and I'm gonna find out exactly how. If he still *is* moving drugs through my company, I'm gonna crucify his ass."

"Still moving drugs?" I repeat. "Abe, I fired Mercee. He's not doing anything here now."

"So he wants us to think," Abe says. "But you caught Eric selling his shit in the break room, so that means Mercee's operation has legs."

"Eric is gone too."

"Yes, but that begs the question: Who else under my roof is working for Irving Mercee?" He sees the shock in my eyes, then reaches across the table and takes my hand. "Me and you are gonna catch Mercee and whoever else is a part of his little scheme. And when we do, I'm gonna make sure none of them ever see the light of day again."

He stares at me with his intense, dark brown eyes, and I'm doing everything I can to keep mine from betraying my truth.

Chapter 13

Abe Gholson, *President of B.N.I.*

As soon as I step on the porch, I bang on the raggedy wood door with a closed fist. I have very little patience when I have to step outside the comfort of my luxurious, temperature-controlled office.

"Who is it?" a voice says through the door.

"Open the fucking door, Mr. Alden," I say.

The door unlocks, then swings open.

I'm face to face with a lanky young man in a white tank top, the hem of it wrinkled up over a pair of dark blue boxer shorts. He rubs his eyes as if he just woke up (even though it's only ten till nine at night), then he lifts a leg and scratches his bony kneecap.

I know this is Eric Alden, the 20-year-old whom Nysha fired for selling weed on my property. I snagged his file from Nicholas Rolfe, and on my way over here I studied his work photo and read through a list of infractions that included tardiness, insubordination, and even a write-up for sexual misconduct (he received a hand-job from a female employee in the break room two months ago). As I look at him now, I wonder what Nysha saw in him that made her want to give him a job in the first place.

"Who are you?" Eric asks, as he gives my solid black textured wool Givenchy suit the once-over.

"You don't know who I am?"

"No," he says irritably. "Am I supposed to?"

"Yes. You used to work for me."

He tilts his head to the side, studying me through narrow eyes. He shakes his head no.

"My name is Abe Gholson."

"Who?"

"I'm the president of Black Nile Industries."

His eyes go wide, as he covers his open mouth with a hand. "Oh shit," he whispers. He drops his hand and reveals a smile. "I didn't know you were black. Am I getting my job back?"

"We need to talk about that first," I say.

"Well come in, sir!"

He hurries into his living room, clearing his coffee table off with the sweep of his forearm, knocking all the table-top trash—empty chip bags, blunt wrappers, QuikTrip cups with gnarled straws jutting out lids, even an ash tray—off into a small trash bin. There are brand new designer clothes with price tags scattered over his couch and arm chair. Eric sees I have no place to sit, so he snatches all the clothes up, stuffing each pair of jeans, each shirt, each embossed leather belt under his arm until most of it is gathered.

Then he tosses it all behind the couch, out of sight.

"Make yourself at home," he says.

I frown. "Impossible."

"Huh?"

"I need to talk to you about why you were fired from my company."

He bites his bottom lip, then plops down on his couch, deflating its cushions. "Nysha caught me selling weed again."

"Again?"

"It wasn't the first time, so I can't blame her for firing me. But I promise, if you give me another chance, I'll never sell weed on your property again. That's my word. I don't play about my word. I apologize for my bad actions, Mr. Gholson. I wrote an apology letter to Nysha ..."

"She didn't tell me about a letter ... Did you already email it?"

"No, it's not an email. I wrote it down on paper."

"Where is it?"

"Right here," he says, as he jumps up and leaves the room.

A moment later he's passing back through the living room, but he disappears into the kitchen, where I hear him rummaging through drawers. "It's around here somewhere," he mumbles. He comes back in the living room, plants his hands on his hips for a moment, looks around discouragingly, then an idea hits him and he heads toward a bedroom.

He's an idiot, I say to myself.

He returns finally, uncrumpling a sheet of notebook paper in front of me. He hands it to me.

"It's not finished," he says. "But most of what I wanted to say is in there."

I start reading:

Dear Nysha, Ur the best boss i ever had. I want to come back to work pleeze. I am sorry for selling drugs. I will not do it again. I miss being around u and Mercee and some of the other crew. Its boring as hell at home. U told me 2 take werk more sirius and thats what I am going to do. Pleeze give me another chance.

"I would've mailed it off already," he mentions, "but I don't have any stamps."

"Lots of new clothes, but no stamps?" I question.

"I don't write letters that much."

It disturbs me that a man like this—no sense of responsibility, no respect for workplace policy—made it into my company in the first place. I wonder if Mercee, an ostensibly great employee, referred Eric to Nysha. I wouldn't doubt that Mercee convinced her to hire him.

"Who do you work for?" I ask Eric, handing him back his letter.

He pauses, and his reply is a question. "You?"

"No, who do you sell weed for?"

"Oh." His forehead creases, then he says, "I don't work for nobody. This is what I do. Weed is my side hustle— *was* my side hustle, if I can get my job back."

"Who do you buy from, Eric?"

He seems hesitant, but then comes forward. "I used to buy from a guy named Don Corey, but I haven't been able to get in touch with him lately. Now I cop from a guy named Antonio Long, from 51st Street."

"I'm giving you a chance to come clean."

"I am, sir. I don't know what you want me to say. I apologize for all of my wrongdoings—"

I punch Eric in the face—a quick, super-swift straight right jab—and his head snaps backwards, the momentum sending him crashing to the floor. It's a punch I practice every weekday morning on a heavy bag, mostly with my personal trainer, Greg. I always thought I'd need this punch for one of B.N.I.'s greedy shareholders, not a low-level employee like Eric.

"I'm tired of fucking with you!" I growl down at him. "Tell me what I need to know about Mercee, NOW!"

Eric touches his nose, sees blood on his fingertips. He looks up at me, astonished. "Mr. Gholson, what was that for?"

"How long have you been working for Irving Mercee?"

"I don't work for him, sir!"

"Wrong answer," I say, as I peel off my suit jacket and throw it on the couch.

"It's the truth, Mr. Gholson. Mercee doesn't sell weed. He never has. He sold cocaine, but that was a long time ago."

I unbutton my shirt sleeves and roll them up to my elbow.

"It's the truth! I asked him if I could work for him but he said no. He's not living that life anymore."

"Who else at B.N.I. is working for Mercee?"

"Nobody, sir. It's not what you think—"

I reach down and clutch him by his neck, yanking him to his feet. I slam him against the wall and throw a body shot to his liver. He buckles over with a painful gag, his ability to breathe devastated.

"I think you and Mercee tried to take advantage of one of my top employees' kind heart," I say to him. "But she caught you muthafuckas. Nysha isn't as dumb as you shitheads think, huh? And you must think I'm dumb if I'm gonna let some ex-con threaten the reputation of a company that took my whole adult life to build."

"Sir ... no," Eric says hoarsely. He holds out a hand to push me away. I grab his arm and twist it behind his back, shoving his face hard against the wall.

Bang.

"No, what?" I snarl in his ear.

"I don't think Nysha is dumb. I like her. I respect her. So does Mercee. And Nysha likes us too, I thought. I know she likes Mercee for sure."

"And why do you think she likes Mercee?"

"Nysha is always asking me questions about him, about what he used to do in the streets. She never asks about anybody else, no other employees but Mercee. I think they're dating. They're always in her office alone, with the door locked."

I spin Eric around, keeping his back pressed to the wall. I loom closer, my nose inches from his, as I point my finger in his face. "Are you lying to me?"

"No, sir. Fuck no. What do I gotta lie for? Ask Nysha."

The possibility that Mercee and Nysha are an item lingers in my mind, along with the far-fetched idea that they were working together to push cocaine through Black Nile Industries. But it just doesn't add up. Why would Nysha risk her career—not to mention her freedom—helping a drug dealer fuck me over? Could she be trying to get back at me because I cheated on her so many times? I can't see it. Not Nysha. She's not a vengeful woman. If she hated me that much, she would have walked out on B.N.I. after our relationship ended.

On top of that, why would she pick a tattooed criminal over a debonair billionaire?

"Liar!" I shout in Eric's face.

"Man, I just want my job back."

"You think I'm gonna let you work for me again? You're out your fucking mind. Tell me what you know about Mercee."

"You can't do this to me. Man, I can sue you for this shit."

I launch my hand out, clawing his neck, trying to crush his windpipe. He chokes for air. "That's what you want, ain't it?" I say seethingly. "You want the easy dollar. You want the good life handed to you on a silver platter. You don't really wanna work for shit. You think I didn't have the opportunity to sell drugs when I was your age? You think you're the only one who grew up without a mommy and daddy?"

His face is turning red. He can't speak, let alone breathe.

"I was an orphan. I had no one. And when all the other teens were sneaking out to go to parties and fuck little girls, I would sneak out to go to the public library. The Lucile H. Bluford branch, 30th and Prospect. Do you know where that is? I bet you don't. The staff at the orphanage still beat my ass every time I got caught sneaking back in, even though the books I had under my arm were time-stamped. They *knew* I was at the library, and *still* busted my lip, blacked my eye. Have you ever been beaten for trying to succeed? For trying to do better for yourself? Probably not, because you don't know what blameless struggle is. I earned what I have today, Eric. And I'm not gonna let you, Mercee, or anybody else—"

Eric headbutts me, driving his rock-hard crown into the bridge of my nose with punishing force.

I'm dazed for a second.

"Got me fucked up," I hear him say.

When my vision clears, I look down to see my own blood spilling onto my necktie, and then I notice that Eric isn't in front of me anymore.

I look to my right.

He's running!

I give chase, as he zips around the corner into the hallway, headed to the rear of the house. Holstered in the small of my back is a five-shot revolver. I yank it out, as I watch Eric race to the back door, encountering a janky door knob that won't turn—precious seconds wasted, to my delight. Finally he thrusts it open and—

Boom!

I fire once. The bullet slams into his upper back and he falls through his screen door and onto his back porch, dead. I swipe my forearm across my nose, leaving a streak of blood on my linen, as I walk up to Eric's lifeless body. I reach down and grab him by his left ankle, then I drag him back inside the house.

Chapter 14

Michael Frisk, *Detective*

After hanging up his phone, Chief Knam plants his elbows on his desk and hides his face in his palms. "Why, why, why?" he says in a muffled moan. Then he runs his hands through strands of gray hair and looks up at me and Copeland with tired eyes.

"What did the prosecutor say?" I ask, knowing it can't be good.

Knam stares at me for a moment, then shakes his head no.

I close my eyes and sigh, as hope drains from my face and settles uncomfortably in my stomach, where it dissipates. Our approval for a wiretap on Nysha Hawk's phone has been denied.

We came to Knam this morning asking for lawful interception—not just a wiretap on her calls, but access to her text messages and cyberspace profiles. After Copeland told Knam that he saw a picture of Nysha and Mercee on her phone's lock screen, the chief didn't have a problem with making a few phone calls to get the monitoring started. First he called a state judge. But as a result of recent, illegal wiretapping from law enforcement in other cities and other states—especially Michigan, where Knam is from—power to grant wiretaps has shifted to federal prosecutors.

"Do you wanna know why the prosecutor denied it?" Knam says in an ominous tone, suggesting that me and Copeland were at fault.

"What did we do wrong?" I ask.

"She told me that she received an email just this morning, CC'd to her and a hundred other government officials in regards to Nysha Hawk and Black Nile Industries. Apparently the owner of Black Nile, Abraham Gholson, whom you guys had a sit-down with, contacted the attorney general and complained that you two violated one of his employees' civil liberties by approaching her at her home."

Copeland's mouth drops. "You're kidding ..."

"But that's standard police procedure," I say in our defense. "We didn't break into her home or try to bully her. She invited us in. She didn't seem to have a problem with—"

Knam silences me with his palms. "Look, I'm not saying you guys broke protocol. I'm just saying that this Nysha Hawk woman has an umbrella of protection from a powerful man who can influence our elected officials with a sour email. In it, Mr. Gholson threatened to move B.N.I.

out of Missouri, which means millions of dollars in taxes headed elsewhere, and Missouri can't afford for that to happen. So no wiretap on Nysha Hawk. I have to ask you boys to leave her alone."

"That's bullshit," Copeland spews.

"It is." Knam leans back into his chair and crosses his arms over his big chest. "But ... Copeland, I have to ask you again: Are you *positive* you saw Mercee on Nysha Hawk's phone?"

"I'm positive, sir."

"How positive?"

"I'd bet my life on it."

Chief Knam stares at him, mulling over a thought. "Well then, there has to be another way to get to Mercee. Who else can we pursue that's connected to him in some way?"

"Brandi Nieman and Zakaria Livingston," I say quickly. "They were his co-defendants. Brandi was Mercee's girlfriend at the height of his drug career, then she turned into an addict, hooked on cocaine. She was distant from Mercee's operation toward the end, but we got a conviction on her and threw her in prison right along with them. She was released several years before the others, and apparently she picked up right where she left off—smoking crack.

"Zaki is the enforcer of the bunch. He's been tied to over twenty homicides in the Kansas City area, and several around the country, but we haven't been able to get one

125

murder to stick." Knam grunts, but I continue. "We almost had him once. We got intel on one of Mercee's drug houses that Zaki oversaw. We decided to raid it early in the morning, but Zaki was ready for us. We were outmanned and outgunned and had to retreat."

Knam shakes his head. "Shameful. That would've never happened if I had been in charge," he says, and leans forward again. "Which one do we want to bring in first?"

"Brandi," says Copeland.

"Yes, Brandi," I second. "We don't have a location on Zaki, but Brandi is on unsupervised probation, so her current address and stipulations are still on file and active. She has to attend rehab every Monday, Wednesday, and Friday. She was supposed to be done with the program years ago but she kept relapsing, getting sent back to prison, then released again, over and over, having to start the program from the beginning each time. From a few letters in Mercee's prison property that me and Copeland read, it's a fact that Brandi wants back in the drug game. Now whether or not Mercee will or has already let her come back to the team ..." I shrug. ".... We can't confirm."

Knam points to the door behind us. "Well, go confirm it," he says.

***

The clock above my fireplace shows 1:15 a.m., as I walk into my home and hang my sport coat up in the closet. This is actually one of the earliest times I've made it home, and too bad my wife isn't here to witness it. She's on vacation with our six-month-old daughter, visiting family in Florida— where I should be too. But ever since we got that anonymous recording with Mercee's voice on it, the last thing I need to ask Chief Knam for is time off.

"Meow."

I look around, not knowing where the sad hello came from. Then I hear it again:

"Meow."

I squat down and see my British shorthair cat, Nikki, laying underneath a dresser in my hallway.

"Nikki, why are you hiding from me?" I say, smiling.

She simply stares at me with wide, copper eyes.

"You look scared. Why are you scared? Or are you just mad at me for coming home late again? Don't be mad. I promise I'll do my best to be home early tomorrow. It's just that things are picking up at work. We went looking for Brandi Nieman today."

Nikki doesn't seem to care.

"C'mere."

Slowly, my furry friend crawls out from underneath the dresser and saunters up to me. She purrs when I scratch

127

her underbelly and pet her dense coat of dark gray. She follows me to my computer room, where I sit and slide out my keyboard. One giant leap and Nikki is in my lap, snuggling there. Her favorite spot.

"Me and Copeland couldn't catch up with Brandi tonight," I tell her, as I type in my password. "We went to her home, knocked on her door, nobody answered. We went to her job, some telemarketing firm in Olathe, Kansas, but they said she quit a week ago. We went to her rehab center after that, but I guess we got there an hour too late. They were closed."

Nikki purrs.

"Yep, bad luck. But tomorrow—or should I say *today*— is a new day."

I type the rehab center's website in the search box and click on the first link. I see a picture and a bio of a man named Wayne Layson. He's an instructor with a couple college degrees. A middle-aged man with thick, neatly braided dreads and a handsome smile. I click on the gallery link and see pictures of him with a bunch of addicts and recovering addicts, including one with Brandi Nieman. He's presenting her with some kind of a sparkly necklace.

This rehab center seems like the best place to approach Brandi. The problem is it's only open every other day, not including weekends, so me and Copeland are going to have to wait until—

Suddenly, my computer monitor flicks off.

"What the heck?"

Then, seconds later, all the lights in my house go out.

"Meow," Nikki says to me in the darkness.

"I know, meow is right."

Moonlight is shining in through a few windows surrounding me, so I can see all around my living room with hardly any problem at all. Nikki jumps off my lap as I stand and walk over to the window at the front of the house, peeking out the blinds to see how many other houses lost power.

I'm surprised to see that every single one of my neighbors' houses within eyesight have lights.

"You're kidding me," I say.

Parked at the curb in front of my house, I notice a vehicle is hidden in shadow. It's big, an SUV maybe, and I don't recognize it as a regular in this area.

Then I see a flash, hear a burst of gunshots, and my window explodes in my face, thousands of pieces spraying into me.

I drop to the floor, glass bits showering my body. Bullets ricochet inside my house. Zipping over my head. I hear my coffee pot shatter. I use my forearm strength to crawl over to my hall closet, where I have an assault rifle stored.

With my head low, stomach pressed to the floor, I reach up and turn the knob—and a bullet slams into the back of my hand!

I grit my teeth to keep from crying out, from giving away my location—*how many assailants are here, am I surrounded?!*—as I cuddle my hand to my chest. A chunk of meat just below my ring finger is gone. Blood spills down my palm into the wrist of my shirt sleeve.

The shooting has stopped.

Then I hear tires screeching out front.

Are my attackers getting away? I hope so. Please let them be gone, I pray silently.

For as long as I can bear the throbbing pain in my hand, I lay still. Then it becomes too much, the pain traveling up my forearm, gnawing into the ligaments supporting my elbow. And as I try to sit up, my shoulder screams. My whole body is on alarm—my limbs tender, every muscle sensitive, begging me not to move.

But I have to. I struggle to my feet, and suddenly the important thing to do is no longer catering to my hand; it's finding—

"Nikki!" I holler.

I trudge through my kitchen, bypassing the bullet holes in the walls, then I go around through my living room, overlooking the debris and the trail of blood drops in my wake, as I search for my shorthaired feline.

"Nikki! Where are you?! Tell me you're okay!"

Then I hear it, loud and beckoning: *"Meow!"*

I follow the sound, dropping to my knees by the hallway dresser, looking underneath it. I see Nikki in the same state as she was moments ago—she's on guard, as if expecting me to crawl under there with her.

My smile is full of relief. "You had the right idea the whole time," I say.

Chapter 15

Irving Mercee, *Cocaine Kingpin*

Nysha sits on my leather couch, crossing her arms as she sinks back into the cushions. I try to hand her a glass of Crown, but she shakes her head no.

She's still upset.

"We both need to be clear-headed if we're going to work through this," she says.

"There's nothing to work through," I say. "Everything is okay."

"It's not okay, Mercee. You keep saying that, but it's not. The cops showed up on my doorstep. We can't even be together at my house anymore because they're watching it. If I wanna be with you, I have to come here all the damn time now."

"What's wrong with my condo?" I ask.

"It's nice, but it's not us. I just hate downtown. I want everything to go back to normal."

I put the drinks back in the kitchen, then come back and sit down next to her. I say, "This is the new normal, Nysha. This is a better us. You'll get used to it. Right now the drugs are on your mind constantly, it has you scatterbrained, because it's not what you're accustomed to. Trust me, the worrying will all gradually go to the back of your mind, and then your nerves won't be so tight. I understand how you're feeling though. I was the same way when I first started selling drugs."

"But Abe Gholson is doing his own investigation too, Mercee. He has a lot of power. He has a lot of connections."

"I do too," I say.

She looks at me doubtfully. "He's a billionaire."

"My connect is a billionaire."

"Yeah, in Mexico. But we'll both be in prison here in the United States. How will his connections help us then?"

I jump to my feet and flip over my coffee table violently, shattering its glass top. Nysha lets out a small scream of fright. I step away from the mess, walking over to the other end of my living room, where I plop down on my chaise lounge. I have to distance myself from her for a moment. I'm not used to women questioning me like this. I'm not used to women who don't believe in me. Both Brandi and Lucille knew how great I was, how easily I could overcome unforeseen events, staying perfectly poised while I work through serious problems. And yes, detectives Frisk and Copeland are serious problems. And yes, I didn't anticipate the owner of B.N.I. taking up his own cause to shut me down. But Nysha is acting like I can't handle it. I handled similar issues as a damn teenager. I handled customers who didn't pay, I handled snitches, I handled the police, I handled prison, I'm handling my fiancée's death—I've handled more shit than Nysha could ever realize.

I look up and see her standing. She slides her purse strap on her shoulder.

"Where you going?" I ask.

"To get some rest," she says. "I have to be at work early tomorrow to train the new hires. I had to hire two more people to replace you and Eric. They're going to be working your zone. I have to make sure they don't mess up a thing, especially the packages coming in from Mexico."

"I thought you were giving up on helping me."

"I never said that. I just want us to be on the same page. Because that's how things go wrong—miscommunication. You know how technical I was at work. I think of the worst possibilities and try to find solutions to them before they happen."

"I do too."

"Well stop trying to fight me every time I ask a tough question."

I open my arms, letting her know I'm willing to hear her thoughts.

"I'll deal with Abe Gholson," she says. "He trusts me. So I'm sure he'll run every step of his investigation by me.

He has so far. I'll make sure none of your cocaine gets discovered during his upcoming probes."

"Thank you," I say.

"But I need you to make sure I know where you are at all times. No way in hell should I be calling you with some important information, only to find out that you just got off a plane in Detroit or anywhere. That's ridiculous."

I nod and say, "I agree. That was foul. With this amount of cocaine coming in, we need to have direct access to each other at all times. I get it."

"No, fool, knowing where you are has nothing to do with cocaine. I'm your girlfriend, remember? Knowing where you are at all times is for my peace of mind."

I smile abashedly. "Oh."

She stares at me for a moment, her face studying mine, and my smile fades. I get the feeling that she's questioning whether or not she can trust me with her heart. It's an unsettling feeling—because I'm not sure if she can.

"Call me tomorrow," she says. "Please? Don't forget me."

I stand up to see her out. We meet at the door and I hold it open for her. Taking her hand in mine, our fingers intertwine as one, almost magnetically. We kiss once. It's a small kiss, respectful, no passion, just a formality.

A wave of guilt washes over me.

"I'm not coming back over here until you get a new coffee table," she says.

I crack a smile, and then I pull her close again and we share a better kiss.

"I'ma do my best to communicate more," I say. "I'm just not used to somebody giving me too much feedback on a hustle that I know backwards and forwards."

"Well get used to it, Mercee," she says. "See ya."

I watch her walk to the elevator, then I shut my door.

Only a few seconds after I turn the lock, I hear Brandi behind me: "That bitch is gonna be the end of all of us if we don't get rid of her."

I turn, as she emerges from my second bedroom with her drink in hand. She looks down at her sheath dress, tugging up its neckline to keep her breasts from spilling out. I head straight to the kitchen, where I pour myself some more apple-flavored whisky. It didn't feel right at all what I just did. I invited Brandi to "meet" Nysha—anonymously. Brandi begged me to show her what type of woman Nysha was, wanting to be sure she wasn't competition. I was against the idea completely, but Brandi made a soft threat that she'd leave the team if I had something real going on with Nysha. "If she's all that, then you don't need me," Brandi had said. So we came up with this idea; I had to "prove" to Brandi that I'm only making Nysha believe we're a couple out of necessity. And Brandi promised on her life that she wouldn't interrupt us—she'd merely spectate and listen in from my second bedroom.

"We can't get rid of her," I reply to Brandi as she enters the kitchen. "Nysha is the most important piece right now."

"I thought *I* was the most important piece." Brandi has a splotch of Crown swirling within her glass. She takes a slow sip. "Hmm?"

"You know what I mean, Brandi. I'm not inside Black Nile Industries anymore. I'm not involved in the day to day. She's our eyes and ears now. She's very necessary."

"I thought you said you and her already put together a system that works by itself. The packages can come and go through B.N.I. undetected all on their own now, right? So what do we need her for?"

"Systems fail, Brandi. We need Nysha to make sure they don't. And you heard what she said about B.N.I.'s president, Abe Gholson. He's launching his own investigation. Nysha is gonna be in there keeping her boss's nose out of our shit."

"How do we know she's not crossing us? She could be helping the investigation."

I pause briefly—rethinking Brandi and her role, but knowing I need her—then I sip some of my drink. "Nysha had the perfect chance to turn me in when she found the drugs and the money at the warehouse. But she didn't. She committed herself to me by taking both boxes off B.N.I. property and making sure she gave them to me safely. So you tell me why she would decide to cross us now?"

Brandi isn't convinced, but she lets it go. She says, "What does Zaki think about her? Does he know that she's aware of the cocaine distribution? You didn't give me a good answer last time I asked you."

"Zaki doesn't know yet."

"Oh." Brandi seems excited to have found out before my righthand man. "You know he's gonna be mad when you tell him. You know he has an extreme gender bias. Or maybe it's just me he hates."

"Zaki doesn't hate you, Brandi. He may not like you, but it's not hate."

"He does hate me, Mercee. He wanted me out of the fold so bad that he laced my weed with cocaine and I didn't find out until halfway through it when I opened it up. I was stupid high and I had to take a peek to see what the shit was. Then he talked me into trying crack when I found out you were seeing Lucille."

"Whose fault was that?"

She rolls her neck. "Lucille was your fault, nigga. The crack was Zaki's fault."

"So you're still blaming the past on everybody but yourself."

Brandi sighs. "No, Mercee. You're right. And I'm not being sarcastic. I kinda pushed you into Lucille. And I had no business spilling my guts out to Zaki. That's part of what I've been learning in this long-ass Milestone program. It's not a hundred percent anybody's fault. We live in an interdependent world, where every choice I make has an influence on someone else. So I have to take responsibility for my own choices," she says. "But Zaki has to take some responsibility too. In his eyes, it's fuck everybody—everybody but you and him. That's how he is. So I know he's gonna be mad when he finds out about Nysha."

"No, he won't."

I leave the kitchen after that, crossing into my living room where I plop down on my couch. I fold my arms in my lap, thinking about tomorrow, about making love to Nysha no matter what our schedules. I owe her an apology, and I plan on apologizing even though she doesn't know she's been wronged. That's what kind of man I am.

Brandi has a seat next to me, in the same spot Nysha was sitting moments ago. She takes the stiletto heel of her ankle boot and crushes a few pellets of scattered tabletop glass, like she's a kid crushing ants, enjoying the soft *crunch* sounds.

"I thought you were going to kill Nysha when you flipped this table. She kept grilling you and grilling you, that dummy. She still thinks she's your boss. If I was you, I would've flipped her ass over." She laughs at her own joke, then finishes off her alcohol. She adds, "And I saw the kisses you gave her. Was the liplocking really necessary, Mercee?"

"She thinks she's my girlfriend, Brandi. I have to kiss her."

"I'm not judging," she says with a smirk. "Okay, actually I am. The first kiss was weak. The second one was so-so, but still weak. So I'm not mad. But I know one thing: She's an idiot if she thinks you really care about her. If a man kissed me like that, I'd know something was wrong."

The way I really wanted to kiss Nysha, the lewd things I really wanted to do to her tonight, would've gave Brandi a heart attack. If she wasn't here, I would've never scared Nysha with that table-flip stunt. That's not me at all (well, that's not me when I'm with Nysha, at least). I had to channel my inner rage to flip that table, and most of that rage came from me knowing I was betraying Nysha by allowing Brandi to spy on us.

I hate when I have to do ugly things to honest people.

"I was a little jealous at first, but I know she's not your type," Brandi decides. "She doesn't know how to go with the flow. She thinks she knows it all. She doesn't realize she's running right into a brick wall with you."

"Seems like you know me best," I say.

"Fifteen years and counting, so I should know." She leans into me, her breasts warm against my shoulder. "Thanks for letting me listen in."

She places a hand on the other side of my jaw, guides my face to hers and kisses my lips. I feel obligated to kiss back at first, but then I start to enjoy her moist lips, and I slide my hand between her thighs. I tell myself that this is just my passion for Nysha being redirected.

Our tongues touch and overlap sloppily. She bites my bottom lip, I wait for her to let go and grab her by the throat, as I push myself on top of her.

I stick my tongue in her mouth.

She sucks it, then lays a big puckering kiss on my lips.

"Now that's how it's done," she grins.

Chapter 16

Wayne Layson, *Rehab Instructor*

Ten minutes till, and I'm trying my best to cum inside of Yee'sha before one of the other girls in class comes knocking on my door looking for me. I'm seated in my office chair, my denims barely hanging on to the top of my knees, as Yee'sha faces away from me, slamming her rear end up and down on my rigid erection.

"*Mmmm*," she moans. "I love your dick, Wayne. Keep it hard for me."

She holds my knees for balance, looks back at me with girlish innocence—this is a game for her, I'm sure—and then she sits in my lap slowly, my manhood disappearing inside her womb.

Then she gyrates.

I tilt my head back, moaning, as my eyes roll in the back of my head. Her warm, pulsing vagina walls have settled my nerves to the point of sedation.

"Don't die on me," Yee'sha says playfully.

She leans against me, her long, rose-scented hair brushing the side of my face. Her gyrations widen and my member bends to her will. I sense that she's done this sex-dance before. It feels too perfect, her erotic moves almost choreographed. But she's amazing nevertheless. I'm short of breath.

"You are truly a woman I admire," I say hoarsely, as I bring my hands around to grope her petite chest. "Yee'sha, I wish you prosperity in your life path."

"You mean that, Wayne?"

"Yes."

"You're not just saying that to keep me wet?"

"I'll never mislead you. Not you or any of the other girls. That's my promise to this program."

"Is this your pussy?"

I don't reply, because she doesn't seem to understand. She must think my words are sex-talk, some passionate hoo-ha that fell out of my mouth unintentionally.

Yee'sha, you don't know me yet, I muse. *But I loved you and your heart and mind before I even met you.*

She bends forward gracefully, her hair falling between my legs as she bounces again. I slide my hand up her spine, raising her shirt in the process, and I grip her by the shoulder. In the middle of her back is a small tattoo of the words "Queen Yee." The font is simple and familiar, but at the tail end of the last "e" in "Yee," the artist lengthened the final stroke into two cheeks that form a tiny heart.

It's this tattoo that spikes my arousal. Yee'sha's self-identity with such a historical word of female strength—not to mention the little heart at the end (a symbol of youthful optimism)—causes me to ejaculate inside of her.

I lift my waist, slightly, if only to go a fraction deeper, and I hold myself here until I have no more semen left to give.

Yee'sha stands up and fixes her shirt. She says, "You're not as great of a lover as everybody thinks you are."

I tug my pants up, looking at her in confusion. "What are you talking about?"

"All the girls in class are always talking about how sexy you are, wondering how good you are in bed. A couple of the girls said they already slept with you and they claimed it was the best sex they ever had in their life."

"Really?"

"Yep. They all think you're a God. They worship you. That's why I came in here. I wanted to see what the big deal was."

As I re-fasten my belt buckle, I recall Yee'sha sending me a text last night, asking me to open class early so I can help her with a few tough questions on her second habit-building worksheet. I was in here showing her example worksheets when she reached around me and grabbed my genitals. I thought Yee'sha just craved attention, as most of the girls do who've lost or detached themselves from their trespassers. They seek male affection, all of them do, and I've been more than happy to be a sustaining source of love (in whatever way they desire), until they find faith and solace in the right partner.

But Yee'sha's motive was clearly different. I was just a mystery to her, a challenge.

"Sorry to disappoint," I say.

"I wasn't disappointed, Wayne." She plucks her worksheet from my desk, rolls it up into a scroll and slips it in her back pocket. "I wasn't blown away by the dick, but I wasn't disappointed either."

She walks to the door, opens it, then turns back to me.

"All my classmates are right about one thing ..." she says.

I tie my dreads back up with a rubberband. "And what's that?"

"You *are* sexy." She winks at me, then leaves my office.

Out of all the information Yee'sha just left me with, what strikes me the most is the gossip among the class. I had no idea the girls spoke so highly of me to one another. *A god,* I think to myself, smiling. *Is that what they really think of me? I just want them to worship themselves, not me. I'm just a catalyst.*

With this in mind, I head out of my office and down the hall, where I can hear the class gathering chairs in the main room. I'm thinking about discarding today's lessons about the stages of drug addiction, and instead touching on the subject of apotheosis, an ideal that can be a disease for women who habitually see their men as greater than themselves.

But when I reach the main room I'm shocked to see everyone standing around Brandi Nieman.

She showed up, I say to myself.

I hear one girl tell Brandi, "You're glowing today. I love your new hairstyle."

"Thank you," Brandi says, as she tries to make her way to the front of the room.

Another girl near her touches a gold bracelet on her wrist. "Did Mercee buy you that?"

"Does Mercee have any brothers?" another asks.

I feel the frustration rising up from my gut. Brandi is not setting a good example for her peers by linking back up with Mercee. And for her to show up here in new jewelry, it advertises a false perception to the rest of the class that trespassers have the ability to reconcile. *If Brandi can make it work with her trespasser, maybe I can too*—I can see this very virus spreading through their thoughts, eating away at their common sense.

I won't tolerate it.

I stand next to the sign-in table, where I know Brandi is heading. She sees me and smiles, and I notice that her bottom row of teeth are capped in pink diamonds.

"Good evening, Wayne," she says.

"What are you doing here?"

She frowns. "You're supposed to say good evening."

I give her a death stare.

She says, "What are you mad at me for?"

"Because I thought you were done with the class," I say. "I thought you were running off into the sunset—or should I say *darkness*—with your trespasser."

She ignores me, fishing a black and gold ballpoint pen out of her purse. This gesture irritates the hell out of me because there's already a pen attached to the sign-in sheet, the same cheap pen everyone's been using for the past three weeks.

Does Brandi think she's too good for us now?

I place my hand flat on the sign-in sheet. "Brandi, you can leave."

"Leave? No, I'm not leaving. Move your hand."

"What's wrong with the pen that's already provided?"

"What do you mean what's wrong with it? *Everything* is wrong with it, Wayne. I got tired of shaking that damn thing over and over to get it to work. And when you do get ink to come out, it bleeds. That pen holds up the line. So I brought my own."

"Why now?"

She shrugs. "I don't know. Does it matter?"

"It matters a whole hellavuh lot, Brandi. You came in here today causing a disruption with your fancy dress and your fancy pink teeth, all high and mighty. Your appearance isn't a good representation of this program."

"I can't be beautiful? You want me to look busted like the rest of these crackhead bitches in this class? I could've wore more jewelry, but I didn't. Mercee bought me a necklace that looks just like this one"—she touches the Milestone pendant hanging from her neck—"but I didn't wear it because I'm dedicated to this class. I'm here today and every day to motivate these girls. I'm giving them hope."

"False hope," I say. "You're telling them it's okay to go back to their trespassers. You're gonna get these women killed."

"I'm not telling them to go back to their trespassers just because I went back to mine. I'm just showing them that all trespassers are not created equal. Mercee has changed. I've changed. The class needs to know that it's possible to make things work in a relationship if there's compromise."

"There is no compromising with a trespasser. You know that, Brandi."

"Mercee is *not* a trespasser anymore."

I stare at her hard. "Get out of my class."

"No, Wayne. I earned my right to be here. You're only trying to kick me out because you're jealous of us. Or because our relationship doesn't fit into your little box of wisdom."

"I'm not jealous," I say adamantly. "I'm saddened by your regression. You have so much potential to be great all on your own, without me or Mercee."

"I'm not leaving this class," she says. "I already know what's going to happen. You're gonna issue a warrant for my arrest for being absent."

"I won't."

"Well let me sign in then."

I move my hand. She scribbles down her name with her gold pen, then clicks it closed.

"Bye," I say.

"I'm leaving. But I'll be back for the next class. You can make me leave again if you want to, but as long as I get to sign in and get my credit, I don't give a fuck."

She starts for the door. The rest of the class stares at her, a few asking where she's going.

"I'm going to ride off into the darkness with my trespasser!" she hollers, her tone chock full of sarcasm. "Yee-haw! I'm out this bitch!" She throws up the peace sign without looking back.

Chapter 17

Michael Frisk, *Detective*

"How long until the class lets out?" Copeland asks me, as we sit in the parking lot of the rehab center, our squad car parked up front with an unobstructed view of the main entrance.

"It just started," I say. "So I think we have another three hours."

I look down at the white cast on my left hand. It's a grave reminder of the attempt on my life, in my own home. There were bullets found lodged in my walls all throughout my house and shell casings found in the street. There were also shell casings found on my front porch and in my bushes, which means the shooter hiked up close to the house. And it was even determined that one of my power lines was severed.

It wasn't a drive-by.

It was a cold, calculated hit.

But a failed hit, thankfully ... other than my hand.

I look over when I hear Copeland strike his lighter. He lights a blunt from the driver's seat, where I'd be sitting if both of my hands worked. I hate when he drives, because he's always under the influence.

He holds the blunt out to me.

I shake my head no. "And you shouldn't be smoking either. You're operating a motor vehicle, Copeland."

"I know. That's why I rolled a low-tolerance strain. This is Plushberry, not my usual Cookies. It has less THC. But it still has those relaxing properties in it, strong enough to give you some pain relief in your hand."

"I'll pass," I say.

"Suit yourself."

I reach over him and press down on all four power window buttons, letting them all down. He laughs and coughs at the same time, but I don't see anything funny about a cop car full of weed smoke in front of a rehab center. I love Copeland, but sometimes ...

"Look!" he says, pointing. "That's her, ain't it?"

I follow his finger, and I see Brandi Nieman for the first time since her federal sentencing over seven years ago. She just pushed out of the front doors, walking in a hurried pace to her car. She looks upset.

"Damn, she got thick over the years," Copeland notes.

"Go get her!" I yell.

He throws his blunt in the ashtray and hops out the car. I watch him jog across the parking lot toward her, holding out his police badge to her. When she sees Copeland approaching, she pauses, looks around as if she's searching for an escape route.

She's about to run!

But Copeland catches up to her before she bolts. I don't know what he said to her, but she hits him with her purse. He grabs her by the arm and ushers her over to our car. He throws her in the back seat, comes around and drops back in the driver's seat. He turns the ignition, starts it up.

"This is illegal!" Brandi fumes. "Where's yall search warrant? What are yall arresting me for?"

"I told yo buckethead ass we got a pickup warrant on you," Copeland says. "You're not under arrest. We're just picking yo stupid-ass up for questioning."

Brandi lurches forward, smacking him in the back of the head.

"Do you want assault on a police officer to go along with this?" Copeland hollers. He lights his blunt up again, hits it a couple times, then holds it back to Brandi. "Here, calm yo ass down."

"No," she says. "I don't smoke no more. I swear you two are the most bored muthafuckas on the planet. Yall don't have nothing else to do but harass me?"

Me and Brandi's eyes meet in the rearview mirror. "Good evening, Brandi," I say. "Nice to see you again."

She looks away, folding her arms. "Hi, Mike."

***

I enter the interrogation room behind Copeland. He's carrying in two cups of water—one for himself and one for Brandi. I have a cup of steaming hot coffee in my hand for myself, blowing the surface with puckered lips as I shut the door with the elbow of my bad hand.

"Congratulations on your sobriety," I say to Brandi, as I have a seat at the table across from her. "Last time I saw you, you were standing before the judge and your orange jumper was hanging off of you like rags. You were rail thin. You may not believe it, but I'm proud to see you alive and healthy-looking. You were headed down a rough road."

She takes a sip of her water. "Thank you," she says.

"But what I'm *not* proud of," I add, "is your return to the drug trade with your criminal friend Irving Mercee."

"I'm not in the drug trade," Brandi says.

"Oh yeah? Well how did you afford such a nice bracelet and all those diamonds in your mouth?"

"I know how to save my money. I have a job."

"Telemarketing firm in Olathe?" I ask.

"Yes."

Copeland says, "We already went there. They said you quit." He's standing against the wall in the corner, half hidden in shadow, with his arms crossed. His hood is pulled up like the grim reaper. "Any more lies you wanna tell, Ms. Neiman?"

"I didn't quit. They fired me. I'm receiving unemployment."

"So you're telling us you bought all of that stuff with unemployment benefits?"

"Yep. Kansas unemployment went up. It's a lot higher than Missouri's." She stares at the camera in the corner of the room, grins, then stares off to the side as if she's outsmarting us.

"Let me tell you what we know," I say. "We know Irving Mercee is selling cocaine again. We know he was working at Black Nile Industries. We know he found a way to move Jose Horrell's cocaine through Black Nile. We also know that his girlfriend and former manager, Nysha Hawk, is helping him traffic his cocaine through the company."

Brandi cuts her eyes at me. I struck a nerve.

"We also know that you and Zakaria Livingston are helping him," I continue. "But what we don't know is exactly how you fit into the equation. If Nysha Hawk is his girlfriend, where does that leave you?"

"You're playing second place again?" Copeland asks her.

"I'm second to nobody," Brandi states.

"It doesn't seem that way," Copeland fires back. "You're notorious for being second place. You were second to Lucille Anthony, weren't you? If I'm not mistaken, Mercee was planning to marry her, not you. And now he has a thing for Nysha Hawk. I can't believe you're putting up with that shit again."

"Fuck you!" Brandi screams. "You don't know what the fuck you're talking about!"

Copeland chuckles. "I think I do. I know a side bitch when I see one."

"Fuck you! I'll never be your side bitch in a million fucking years!"

"You're right. I don't fuck crackheads."

Brandi jumps to her feet. "Keep trying me, muthafucka! I'll cut your fucking throat!"

"Ms. Nieman, sit down," I say. She meanmugs my partner, then plops back down in her seat. "Don't let Copeland get to you. Just focus on answering my questions. You have my permission to ignore him."

Brandi crosses her legs and folds her arms again.

I show her my cast. "Somebody tried to take my life the other night and I think you know who did it."

She's still shooting an icy glare at Copeland.

"Look at me, not him," I say. She turns to me. "Who shot up my house?"

"I don't know," she says.

"Did Mercee order the hit on me because he knows we're getting close?"

"I don't know," she says again. "I doubted. I've never known Mercee to stir up trouble like that unless he absolutely has to. My guess is that you guys pissed some other criminals off." She looks at Copeland again. "Pissing people off is something you guys do best."

"Brandi," I say, "if you add up what we've just shared with you—and factor in what we haven't told you about this investigation—I'm sure you can figure out that Mercee's days are numbered. He's made too many mistakes already, and he hasn't even been out a year yet. So by this time next year, he's gonna be back to doing push-ups in a six-by-eight prison cell. Unless you wanna be in prison with him, I suggest you give us all the help that you can. I don't understand why you have so much loyalty to Mercee and he has zero loyalty to you."

"I don't have loyalty to nobody," she says. "All I do is go to my classes. I'm not doing drugs anymore, I'm not selling drugs, and I haven't seen Mercee in years."

"We've read a few prison letters you sent to Mercee," Copeland reveals. "We know you still want to be with him. We know you were visiting him and bringing him in drugs."

"If yall knew all that and it was true," Brandi says, "then why haven't yall arrested us yet?"

"Where does Mercee live?" I ask her.

"I need a lawyer," she says.

"Is that the route you wanna take?"

"I want a lawyer," she repeats.

I look back at Copeland. He comes forward, pulling Brandi out of her chair by her arm.

"Let go of me!" she screams. "What are you doing?!"

"You're going to a holding cell," Copeland says. "C'mon. Stop resisting."

"What am I under arrest for?!"

"Parole violation."

"I didn't violate shit. I've been doing everything I'm supposed to do out here. You fuckers pulled me out of my rehab class. This is bullshit!"

I watch Copeland haul her away, then turn back to my notes. I had planned to show Brandi copies of her own letters that she sent to Mercee, and tell her that when all of this comes to an end, her own handwriting will be used against her in court. But we didn't get a chance to make it that far because she shut down on us.

Her loss.

With Brandi still having parole obligations, she's in no position to play the tough girl role. We have a right to hold her. Chances are Brandi will be heading back to prison on violation for simply being a part of our investigation. And if that's not enough to have her violated, we can always tack on her assault on Copeland back at the rehab center, or the threat she hurled at him a few minutes ago that we have on camera. We'll make sure Brandi has to finish the rest of her sentence in jail. And while she's sitting, maybe she'll have a change of heart and decide to help us.

I used to have a soft spot for Brandi, which is why I didn't mind her receiving less federal prison time than Mercee and Zaki. I felt like she had already gotten dealt a bad hand with her addiction. And she'd been distanced from

Mercee and his empire at the time the indictments were handed down. But as I look at the cast on my hand—having to endure twinges of pain that shoot through my fingers every half hour—all sympathy for Brandi has vanished.

She can rot in jail just like the rest of them.

Chapter 18

Wayne Layson, *Rehab Instructor*

If only she had listened to me she wouldn't be sitting in a jail cell right now, losing her self-control.

I still have my deluxe headphones on, volume halfway because Brandi is yelling at a detective.

"Let me out of here! Come back here, Copeland! Yall can't do this shit to me! I didn't even do shit!"

"I'll let you out when you're ready to cooperate," Copeland calls back.

A short time passes and I hear Brandi whimpering. I turn the volume up. She's crying. She utters a few words, scolding herself:

"Dammit, Brandi. You're back in here. You said you would never come back here, but you're here. Dammit!"

I hate to listen to my top student beat herself up like this, but she did it to herself.

I made it here in time to listen to Brandi's interrogation because Cynthia DuLord saw the cops arrest her in the parking lot. I asked Cynthia to take over the class for me while I went to see what was going on. I've been sitting here outside of the precinct for two hours now, and through the microphone in Brandi's necklace I was able to hear her defend herself against the detectives with flat-out lies (which they caught her in, more than once), half-truths, and foolish loyalty to her trespasser—everything a Milestone girl *isn't* supposed to stand for.

The good thing about Brandi's arrest is the impression it left on the other girls in the class. Most of them hurried outside after me, and we all witnessed a black detective in a hoodie drag her by her arm across the parking lot, shoving her in the backseat like a wild animal.

"This is what happens when you go back to your trespasser, ladies," I had said to everyone who was standing outside. "Get a good look. Make sure you don't make the same mistake."

Now, as I close my eyes and listen closely to the sounds streaming in my headphones, I try to block out everything but the drum of Brandi's heart, which is beating triple time.

She's afraid.

And she should be.

I hear movement next (she's walking), then the familiar *clack* of a payphone being lifted off of its hook. She's calling someone.

And a few seconds later my cell phone, which is sitting in the passenger seat, alights and starts ringing. Brandi is calling *me*.

In her time of need, she called me first. Not her trespasser.

There's still hope!

I snatch my headphones off, grab my phone and put it up to my ear. "Hello?"

"Wayne, I need your help," Brandi cries.

"What's wrong?"

"I'm in fucking jail."

"What?" I say, smiling at my poor acting. "But you just walked out of class like an hour ago. What did you do?"

"Nothing, Wayne! I swear. Those fucking pigs were waiting on me to walk out of class. They didn't even charge me with nothing. Now they're talking about having my parole violated. If they do that, then I'm fucking screwed."

"Yep, you will be. You'll have to start my program over from the beginning when you get out."

"That's why I need your help."

"I don't understand. Mercee is too busy to help you out?"

"I'm not even thinking about Mercee right now. I don't care about Mercee. I called you because I know you can help. I haven't called anybody else."

"I don't know, Brandi. I mean ... what do you expect me to do? You have to live with your own choices."

"Wayne, *please*! I'm begging you. I'll do whatever you want. I know you have a good relationship with my parole officer. You told me that you two go to lunch together often. You can convince her not to violate me. You can tell her what really happened; I was harassed while at the rehab center. I was doing what I was supposed to be doing."

"But you weren't. You were leaving."

"You told me to leave!"

"Yes, but a Milestone girl should have assessed the problem and took corrective measures. If I was you, I would've removed my diamonds and put them in my car. That's all you had to do. But no, you chose to leave. Now it looks like the police are gonna be removing your jewelry for you."

"I fucked up, Wayne. Is that what you wanna hear? You were right. Going back to my trespasser was the worst thing I could have ever did. I should know better."

"I only wanna hear it if it's the truth."

"It *is* the truth!" she hollers. "Wayne, please make this go away. I'm downtown, 11th and Locust. I don't have a bond so you're the only one who can convince these people to let me go."

"Brandi, there's nothing I can do right now. I have a class to run. I can't neglect the girls who chose to stay, for one who chose to leave."

"But I'm Milestone status."

"And that makes it even worse."

She goes quiet for a moment. I open my glove compartment box, where my address book sits. I flip through it, finding Brandi's name toward the end of the B-tab. Underneath Brandi's information I also have her parole officer's info listed—office number, personal cell phone number, email address, birthday, and even dominant emotional disposition (I have Brandi's P.O. pegged as "friendly, but strict"). I fold the pocketbook backward within itself, saving the page, then I set it in my passenger seat.

"Just come get me when you can," Brandi says in a defeated tone.

"I can't promise you when that'll be," I say. "Office hours aren't till eight tomorrow morning. And then there's no guarantee you're parole officer will listen to me. I've stuck my neck out for you too many times as it is."

"Just try, Wayne. Please?"

"And that's all I ask of you."

I hang up with Brandi, then shove all of my recording apparatus off my lap and start up my Passat. I'm still not sure if I'm going to call her parole officer on her behalf. I just might request that she sit there for six months to a year. It's a chance that it could very well save her life.

Chapter 19

Irving Mercee, *Cocaine Kingpin*

I flip to the back of the menu, scanning the list of spirits with my finger. I have no idea what I want to sip on. It's hard for me to think straight at the moment. So much shit on my mind. "Surprise me," I say to the waitress, exasperated.

"And you?" she asks Zaki.

"Something red," Zaki says. "Anything red, thank you."

The waitress scribbles on her notepad and smiles at us. "Here at the Bristol, one of our house specials is the Atlantic Salmon with bourbon maple glaze. All of our salmon is fresh and broiled to give it a golden, crispy crust—"

"Just get our drinks," Zaki interrupts. "We got urgent business to discuss. Go, scoot off."

The waitress's cheeks turn red with embarrassment. "Sorry. Your drinks will be right out," she says, and quickly stalks away.

"You're a piece of shit when it comes to women," I say to Zaki, shaking my head.

"You're one to talk, *playboy.*" He reaches in his coat pocket and pulls out a business card, placing it on the table. He puts a finger on it and slides it across to me.

I read it. "Express Car Wash?" I say, confused.

"Turn to the other side."

I flip to the back, seeing that Zaki has written down a name.

Antonio Long.

"Who is this?" I ask.

"He's the man we've been looking for. He owns that car wash on the front of the card. He's washing cars and washing his drug money. This whole time I thought it was Don Corey that killed Lucille. Nope, it's him." Zaki points at the business card I'm holding. "Antonio Long. He's our man."

"How do you know?"

"The streets been talking."

"It seems like the streets been wrong," I counter. "What about Boodi Man? What about Don Corey? What about all the niggas you killed before I got out?"

"Hey, I'm just going off what people are saying. For all I know, all these niggas are in cahoots. They all want our position."

"Of course these niggas wanna be on top. Who doesn't? But my concern is Lucille. Did Antonio Long have anything to do with my fiancée's murder?"

Zaki nods his head yes. "He owns a truck like the one that was used to run Lucille off the road."

I lean forward, my heart racing. "Are you serious?"

"This is our nigga," he says. "All roads point to him. Rumor has it, he's been bragging about killing her. He's going around saying he watched her try to kick out the windows until the water rose over her head. He's saying you're too far removed from the game to do anything about it."

I recall what the media reported about Lucille's death. Most of them ran with the Greenville police's account and wrote articles in the context of bad weather and an accidental drowning. And the ones that hinted at foul play never mentioned that Lucille fought for her life.

Antonio Long, I say to myself, trying to remember if I know him from my past. *Antonio Long. Antonio Long.* The more I repeat his name, the harder it is to grasp at a memory that I might be overlooking.

"Go ahead, do it," I tell Zaki. "You got the green light."

"I already know where to find him. We just need to pick a day when you're free, so we can pick his ass up."

"You need me on this one?"

"Yes," he says, as if I insulted him. "We're a two-man team. Mercee and Zaki. When did it change?"

"There's a lot going on, bro. I have some things I need to straighten out."

"Like what?"

"Like Brandi," I say. "I got a call from our lawyer. She got picked up last night and brought in for questioning. They're holding her with no bond and—"

"What the fuck did I tell you?" Zaki curses, pounding a fist on the table, exciting the cutlery and a few nearby patrons. "That crackhead bitch was gonna be our downfall. Didn't I tell you that shit? You're so busy tryna be player of the year and you're gonna end up being inmate of the *century.* I'm not going down with you this time. You're my brother, but fuck that."

"Calm down, Zaki. Brandi isn't even talking."

"What makes you think that shit?"

"Because that's why they're keeping her. She won't talk so they're not gonna let her go. They're gonna violate her parole and make her do her back-up time. She's gonna be off the streets for the better part of the year."

"Good for her," Zaki says.

"No, it's not. Because now I have to work on replacing her. And there's only one person right now that can do it."

Zaki smiles. "Me?"

"No," I say. "Nysha Hawk."

He lets out a chuckle. "You're out of your fucking mind, Mercee. The minute she finds out you're still a drug dealer, she's gonna call the cops."

"No, she won't."

"She will!"

"She won't, Zaki. You wanna know how I know? *Because she already knows*," I say, and I give him a moment to let it sink in. "While we were in Juarez, she found a box of our cash and cocaine at the warehouse. She knew immediately that it was mines, so she took it home to keep it safe and gave it back to me when I got home. She's loyal. We can trust her, probably more than we can trust Brandi. Who do you think has been handling our packages at B.N.I. since I got fired?"

"You said the system can run itself."

"It can, but Nysha is making sure that system stays in place. I haven't told you yet, but her boss, Abe Gholson, is investigating my time of employment there. Detectives Frisk and Copeland somehow got some information that I was moving drugs through B.N.I. I really don't think they know for sure; they're just guessing. But we got Nysha in there making sure her boss and everybody else keeps their asses away from our packages."

Zaki stares at me, his face void of expression. Then he stands up and walks past me. I grab his arm but he yanks it loose.

"Fuck off me, nigga."

"Zaki!" I call, as I watch him leave the restaurant.

I throw a fifty-dollar bill on the table and race after him. I catch up with him outside, at the corner of 14th and Walnut. He was about to walk right through the crosswalk without waiting for the safety countdown, showing no regard for the heavy afternoon traffic.

He turns and looks at me menacingly. "I don't understand, Mercee. It seems like these bitches know more about what's going on within the organization than I do. I'm starting to think you trust them more than you trust me."

"That's not true," I say. "You know we go way back, all the way to grade school."

"Well, why can't I be more involved in the politics?"

"Are you really asking me that, Zaki? You know why. That's not your field. You're too reckless?"

"Reckless? How the fuck am I reckless?"

"I'll tell you why. Because of the shit you just pulled the other day. Did you think I wouldn't find out? It's been all over the news. They keep repeating the shit. You tried to kill Detective Frisk. You shot up his house. Don't lie to me. I know that was you. It had your name written all over it."

"Yes, it was me. But how is that reckless?"

"You're bringing the heat down on us! I don't need to be worried about Brandi and Nysha, I need to be worried about you! You're doing drive-bys on the police."

He gets in my face. "For one, it wasn't a drive-by. That's not how I work and you know it. For two, it wasn't reckless. I cut his power after he got home. I waited for him to come to the window—and I let him have it. I even walked up on the porch and fired inside, up close. I swept the whole room. Yes, I missed him. But it wasn't a drive-by."

"I don't care what it was. You shouldn't have did it."

"Nigga, don't you tell me what I should and shouldn't do," he snarls. "I'm helping us. You're hurting us. I'm putting fear in those cops, just like I did when they tried to raid our dope house. After that, they were so in a rush to arrest us that they made mistakes, they broke the law trying to get a conviction on us. Our lawyer was able to point that shit out in court, and we got less time because of the work that I"—he pats his chest—"put in. Me, Zakaria Livingston. I'm doing everything I can to keep us on track and you're sticking dynamite on the rails with these worthless bitches you keep supporting. I'm tired of it, Mercee. I'm fucking tired. When are you gonna be done acting like you're not just like me? This dream you have of falling in love is gonna be the death of you. Mark my words."

He turns and crosses the street. A car honks at him and he flips his middle finger at it.

"Where are you going, Zaki?" I say aloud.

"To go do some more reckless shit," he says without looking back. "By myself."

Chapter 20

Nysha Hawk, *Manager*

I'm so conflicted, I don't know what to do. I decide to shut my television completely off, sit down on my bed and stare at the black screen, telling myself that there has to be some other explanation.

Irving Mercee can't be responsible. He can't.

When I first heard that Eric Alden had been murdered, I was in the breakroom at Black Nile Industries. I overheard employees talking about how he was shot to death in his apartment over drugs. I immediately pulled out my phone and went to the internet, typed in his name and the story popped up. It was true. Eric Alden had been killed in an apartment complex in south Kansas City, allegedly over a drug dispute.

I had to leave the breakroom before I fell apart. I'm not used to murder hitting so close to home. I trained Eric, taught him how to drive a forklift and interpret B.N.I. scanners and shipping labels. He was just a child.

I sat in my car in the parking lot and cried for a long time. I couldn't help but feel guilty. If I wouldn't have fired him, maybe he would still be alive. At the time he was murdered, he would have been at work or just leaving work.

When I got home I cut on the news and let it be background noise, as I showered and slipped into a pair of blue jeans and a thin undershirt. I was expecting to catch a live story on Eric Alden and more details surrounding his case. What I *wasn't* expecting was the man that actually appeared on my screen.

A reporter was holding a microphone to Detective Michael Frisk, as he answered questions with surprising calm, considering a bullet had disabled his hand during a shooting at his own house. He was sitting next to the reporter on his front porch, his hand wrapped in clean white surgical gauze, stroboscopic flashes of blue and red police lights casting a gloomy illumination on the pre-recorded interview.

"This wasn't a random act of violence," Frisk had said to her. "I was targeted by a coward. And he's going to feel the full force of our department's resources until we have him behind bars."

"It sounds like you have a possible suspect in mind," the reporter said.

I was held in stunned silence, waiting for my boyfriend's mugshot to appear on the screen. A tagline scrolled across the bottom that read: *KC Detective Has Violent Close Call.*

"We have *suspects* in mind," Frisk corrected her.

"It was more than one shooter?"

"I can't be certain. But I do know that even if it was a single shooter, there's more people involved. I believe this attack stems from a current investigation. We're coming close to making a historical bust and the criminals responsible for this are getting scared."

Following the interview, the broadcast jumped to a story on local missing persons and I watched it until the next commercial, then I shut it off.

Now, as I stare at my reflection in the blank screen, I see a troubled woman frozen in thought. My brain's circuits push conflicting information and emotions back and forth, all around my skull, at rapid speeds that start to stir up a headache. Was Eric Alden working for Mercee? *No,* I tell myself. But Abe Gholson sure thought so. What if Abe was right? How certain can you be that Eric wasn't a part of Mercee's crew? Mercee kept secrets from you before, who's to say he still doesn't have secrets? Who's to say Mercee didn't kill Eric to keep him from talking to the police?

"No," I say again, this time out loud to better convince myself.

But after watching Detective Frisk recount his own near-death experience on the local news, it leaves me grappling with a reality that is hard for me to come to grips with.

There's an evil side to Mercee that he's hiding from me. I don't know if I'm safe with him. Is it only a matter of time before he sees me as a threat too?

Even with these thoughts weighing on me, I feel I owe him a chance to explain himself, because there's still an overwhelming part of my soul that is clinging to the belief that he truly loves me.

Reaching in my pocket, I pull out my phone and send him a text, asking him to call me as soon as he can.

He calls immediately.

"Everything all right?" Mercee asks me.

"No."

"What is it?"

"I've been watching the news," I say.

He's silent for an almost imperceptible second, but I take notice. He knows exactly what I'm talking about.

But he asks, "What happened on the news?"

"I saw Detective Frisk on there. Somebody did a drive-by on his home. Somebody tried to murder him."

"Are you serious?"

"I wouldn't joke about something like that, Mercee."

"You sound a little upset about it."

"Frisk was just at my house a few days ago. They could be looking at us as suspects. Frisk said he thinks the people who did it are already under investigation. Who else could he be talking about but us?"

"He could be talking about a million other mutha-fuckas, Nysha. They have stacks and stacks of case files. The KCPD has more enemies than they can keep track of."

"Did we do it?" I ask him flat out.

"Do what? Try to take Frisk out? No, Nysha, why would I do that? You know I'm smarter than that. I'm focused on making sure these last few months go smoothly, so we can be done and move on with our lives, together. I'm not trying to make our situation harder by killing a mediocre detective."

That's what I wanted to hear. Thank you, Mercee.

"Can I ask you about something else?" I say. "And can you give me an honest answer?"

"No. I have to go, Nysha. We'll link up later."

"Did you have anything to do with Eric Alden's murder?" I say quickly.

"Eric who?"

"Eric," I say. "Eric from Black Nile Industries."

"The kid? He was killed?"

From Mercee's tone, it sounds as if he is genuinely just finding out.

"Why the fuck would you think I had something to do with that?"

"Was he working for you?" I ask.

"Hell no. Nysha, what is wrong with you? Are you just sitting around watching the news, trying to pin every murder you see on me? What type of nigga do you think I am? Eric was my young work homie, just like he was yours. He didn't work for me. He worked for you. Look, Nysha, I don't have time for this shit. I got a whole police force trying to pin a bunch of shit on me. I don't need you joining in on the fuckery too. You're supposed to have my back."

"Mercee, I'm sorry. But you have to understand that a lot of stuff is starting to hit close to home and—"

"No, *you* have to understand that I got a lot of shit on my plate and I don't need you sending me text messages, asking me to call you to talk about *bullshit*. You're wasting my fucking time right now! I just had Zaki walk out on me. I got a call from my lawyer earlier, telling me a key player on our side is locked up and won't be getting out no time soon. I might not ever know for sure who killed my fiancée. And I have you flinging nonsense at me, seems like every other day. Ever since I met you, you've been questioning me. I'm starting to think that Zaki is right about you—"

I hang up on him. Me and Mercee have had disagreements throughout our relationship, but he's never bashed me like that before.

My phone rings suddenly; it's Mercee calling me back. I don't know if he's trying to apologize, or him wanting to lay into me more. But because I don't want to hear any more of his anger unravel, I power off my phone.

I think he just needs a chance to cool down.

And I think I do too.

I crawl under my covers with my jeans still on, resting my head on my pillow. I run a mental count of all the packages of Mercee's cocaine that I monitored this week, each box that safely slid through B.N.I.'s sophisticated system, undetected. I fall asleep before I reach a hundred.

***

Thump, thump.

I awake with a start, bolting upright. I heard a strange noise downstairs. I look around my room, my eyes barely able to make out any details in the darkness—except the digital clock on my nightstand, which is erroneously flashing twelve noon, as if it has just been reset.

Was there a power outage?

My whole body tenses when I hear it again:

Thump, thump. Creeaak.

I know those sounds. It's the sounds my wood deck makes when I walk across it. Somebody—*or something*—is in my backyard!

Throwing my covers aside, I swing my feet out of bed and pace over to my window, the one that overlooks my backyard and the neighbor's. I shove it up and a cold draft sweeps in.

I'm shocked when I look down and see a man standing on my deck, his hands cupped against the glass of my back door as he peeks inside my kitchen.

"Are you lost?" I holler down.

He looks up, startled. I'm staring at the face of my boss and ex-boyfriend, Abe Gholson. He smiles up at me.

"I don't think so," he replies. "Does Nysha Hawk live here?"

"I have a front door, you know."

He points beyond the boundary of my fence line. "I saw somebody snooping around your house. So I came around here to the back and they took off running, hopped that fence right there."

"The only person I see snooping around my house is you."

"I tried to call you but it kept going straight to voicemail. I thought something might be wrong. Are you okay?"

I glance back at my nightstand and see my phone, realizing that I shut it off before I fell asleep. I turn back to Abe. "Give me a second," I say.

I comb my hair in the bathroom mirror and then brush my teeth, while trying to figure out what the owner of Black Nile Industries is doing at my house.

What time is it?

Did he find something amiss at work?

I power on my phone; it shows it's closing in on eleven-thirty. It's almost midnight. I also see that I have lots of missed calls and voicemail notifications from Abe and Mercee.

I head downstairs and open my back door. Abe steps inside and hands me a bouquet of pink roses tied together with a reflective pink ribbon.

"What's this for?" I ask.

"For your hard work and dedication at B.N.I.," he says. "This is to let you know that you're greatly appreciated. Your commitment hasn't gone unnoticed."

"Thank you, Abe. But normally we honor our employees once a year at Bartle Hall. When did we start doing house calls?"

"This is a special occasion."

I pull a glass vase from an upper cabinet, then fill it with faucet water and slide the roses inside.

"Your power went out?" Abe asks me.

"Huh?"

He taps the clock on my microwave. It's flashing twelve noon, just like my clock upstairs.

"I guess it did," I say.

Abe asks for a glass of wine and I pour him some pink moscato. I stick the bottle back in the fridge.

"You're not gonna drink with me?" he asks.

"I can't drink alcohol at this time of night. I have to work in the morning."

"No, you don't."

"I know my schedule, Abe. I do have to work."

"I had Nicholas Rolfe go in and override your schedule. You're off for the next three days. Paid, of course." He smiles.

I press my lips together firmly. This is the side of Abe that I always hated. He takes it upon himself to play with your time to suit his fancy. Once, when we were dating, I told him no to sex one night because of a rumor that he was sleeping with another manager at B.N.I. He corrected the situation in his own self-serving way, choosing to have Nick

temporarily switch me to the night shift, working me six—
sometimes seven—days straight. I found out that it was the
opposite shift of the manager that Abe was cheating on me
with. He wanted to keep us apart and keep us busy.

Abe will try to control every aspect of your life. Not
just me, his ex, but all of his employees.

"Sit down and chat with me for a moment," Abe says.
"I won't keep you long. Besides, I paid for everything in this
house anyway."

"I *worked* for everything in this house, Abe."

"Sure you did. And that's why I'm here. To show
appreciation."

We sit down in my living room. I rest my elbow on the
arm of my couch, propping my head up lazily on my fist. I
have no problem telling him through body language that I'd
rather be sleep.

"Nicholas Rolfe and I have finished our internal investigation on Irving Mercee," Abe says. "We have results."

"And they are?" I ask.

"Nothing showed up. Absolutely nothing. We ran
through the system, starting all the way back to Mercee's
start date, looking for packages that were canceled out or
tagged 'lost' in his zone; you know, packages that he might
have taken off the shelves himself and carried home. But
from what we saw in the system, all of his loads checked
out clean. No faults. No tampering. Not even any customer

inquiries about missing or mishandled property, at least not anything out of the ordinary."

"I'm glad to hear that."

"Me too."

We stare at each other for an awkward moment. He smiles. I don't.

"I have to get some sleep, Abe."

"Don't we all?" He gets up, moves to my couch and sinks down next to me. His cologne is light and airy, with a subtle hint of fresh-cut ginger. "This whole investigation has been bothering me since it landed on my desk. Now that it's all resolved, I wonder what it was all for. And I think I figured it out." His arm stretches behind me, resting on the top of the couch. "You wanna know what I came up with?"

"What, Abe?"

"You," he says.

"Me what?"

"You. Us. Think about it, Nysha. How long has it been since we've seen each other? Two, three years? This investigation brought us back together. Don't you believe in fate?"

"You know I believe in fate, Abe. But if you came over here thinking that we were gonna rekindle something, then you better leave now."

"You're seeing someone?"

I pause, then say, "I don't feel comfortable discussing my personal life with you."

"When the fuck did you start feeling uncomfortable?" he spits, snatching his hand from behind me. "I know you still have feelings for me, or you would've quit working for me a long time ago."

"Abe, I'm still working at B.N.I. because it's a great company with a lot of great people."

Except you, I think to myself. Abe is an egotistical man. He puts himself first, always. But in the world of business, his temperament is gold. His arrogance and stubborn belief in himself drove him to create a billion-dollar company with the largest order-fulfillment warehouse in the Midwest. Sometimes he gets in his own way. But his saving grace is knowing how to hire the right people.

"I have a lot of friends and close associates at B.N.I.," I add. "I didn't want to give that up just because I had to give you up. And it's a big location. It's world headquarters. We never have to see each other, so it was an easy decision to stay. I never had intentions of us getting back together."

"You're full of shit," he says. "You love me still. I know you do."

I glare at him. But before I can respond, I hear a knock at my front door and I jerk my head around. I see a shadow through my sheer blue curtains, someone standing at my doorstep after midnight.

I know who it is.

My heart starts beating faster. I almost feel like I'm suffocating.

"Expecting someone this late?" Abe asks.

"No," I say. "Wait here, please."

I get up and walk to my front door anxiously. I open it up halfway, staring into Irving Mercee's eyes with nervous fright, as I squeeze outside and close the door behind me. Mercee is wearing a gray trench coat with a black infinity scarf, his gold Rolex timepiece twinkling under my dim porch light—a look more elegant and regal than I've ever seen Abe in. Mercee has a single-stem red rose cradled in his arm. The cellophane crinkles as he gives me a hug.

He reads my expression. "You're still upset with me?" he says.

"Mercee, what are you doing here?"

"I came to see you. To apologize for my language on the phone. I was frustrated and it came out on you. It's not you I'm upset with, it's everybody else."

"We agreed that I'm only supposed to visit you downtown. It's not safe for you to be here until the whole criminal investigation is officially over."

"I know. I tried calling you but you didn't answer your phone. I didn't want to end my night on bad terms with you. I took a chance coming here, but you're worth that chance. And I didn't see any detectives in the area anyway. Definitely not on this street. We're good, don't worry. It's cold, can we go in?"

Outside barefoot, breath vapors clouding, a chill passes through me and I shiver, but more out of anxiety than

Mercee's reminder of the low temp. I glance inside through my curtains. I can't see if Abe is still sitting on my couch or not. I point to the Mercedes-Benz G-Wagen parked at the curb and Mercee looks.

"Whose is that?" he asks.

"Abe Gholson!" I say in hushed excitement.

His face turns into a mask of confusion, as he cuts his eyes to my living room curtains, hardly able to see a thing beyond the sheer material. He eyes me curiously. "What's your boss doing here this late?"

I open my mouth to speak—then the door behind me squeaks open. I feel paralyzed when I hear Abe's hard voice.

"I just came by to thank one of my top employees for a job well done," says Abe.

I look at Abe's face and see profound composure. It's his game face, a fake persona of civility that I've seen him put forward in manager pep talks and employee-of-the-month celebrations.

"You must be the infamous Irving Mercee. My name's Abraham Gholson. It's nice to finally meet you." Abe extends his hand.

Mercee jams his hands in his coat pockets, rejecting the offer. I have a strong feeling that there's a small handgun on Mercee's person, and I silently pray that it stays concealed. Abe's eyes flick down for a faint second—assessing the possibility of danger, I assume—and he drops his hands to his front, one hand crossing over wrist. It's a guarded posture.

But Abe still smiles. "I take it that you're unhappy that you're no longer working for me. No hard feelings, I hope. After all, your *girlfriend* here—" He says the word *girl-friend* with well-aware emphasis, as his arm slides around my waist. "—is the one who let you go, not me. She's a great judge of character. A great person, period, *inside and out,* if you know what I mean."

He kisses me on the cheek, slowly removes his arm.

"I have to get on my way," Abe says to us both. "I hope you two have a wonderful night. Please enjoy it. Nysha, I'll see you after your three-day vacation. Thank me later. And Mercee..." He pauses, his smile widening as he stands toe to toe with my cocaine kingpin. "You can put that little cute flower inside the vase in the kitchen, with the *thick* bouquet of pink roses that I already gave her. There's room inside, but not very much. I stuffed it full." He winks, then trots down my porch steps and casually strolls over to his Benz.

Mercee casts a look of ice at me, as if he can strangle me right now in the cold.

I have a lot of explaining to do.

Chapter 21

Abraham Gholson, *President of B.N.I.*

I honk twice as I pull away from Nysha's house, my white G-Wagen making a quiet retreat into the night. I keep the phony smile on my face until I'm out of their field of vision, then I take my thumb and click the phone button on my steering wheel.

The voice recognition system prompts me to select a contact.

"Nicholas Rolfe," I say angrily.

The system dials the number for me, and after a brief wait we're connected.

"Abe, what are you doing up so late?" asks Nick, his voice groggy.

"I'm investigating."

"Why do I have the feeling that you've made a discovery?"

"Because I have."

"The Irving Mercee case?"

"Unfortunately, yes."

"What else could there be, Abe? We scoured all the data in our operating system and subsystem since Mercee's start date. We had our night shift scan almost every label in the warehouse, and we even illegally opened up a few international packages. Everything checked out. What could you have possibly stumbled upon at this time of night?"

"Nysha," I say.

"Nysha Hawk? What about her?"

"She's dating Irving Mercee. They're working together to try and bring us down."

I hear flat sheets ruffling on the other end of the line, Nick finally deciding to sit up in bed. He says, "I thought you didn't believe Eric Alden's last dying words, that Nysha and Mercee were in a relationship."

"I didn't. Until now."

I fill Nick in on what just happening, telling him how I had simply come over to show Nysha some gratitude, only to find out that she's sleeping with the enemy. I give Nick my take on the situation: Nysha has access and the know-how to digitally obscure any illegal activity going on in our system, she's helping him traffic his drugs through B.N.I. to get back at me for cheating on her, and this is her screwed-up way of getting my attention.

"I come from a different generation," Nick says. "My wife and I have been together thirty-three years. She got my attention at prom by showing me her girdle, not by trying to undermine a global company that I built from the ground up."

I laugh. "It's a new era, Nick. These new women are firecrackers."

"Obviously." He sighs. "How do you want to handle this? We have to take a totally different approach than how you handled Eric Alden. That was a mess. It took a lot of work to get that to look like a drug-related murder."

"I don't want to kill Nysha. She still loves me, and I still got a thing for her too. I wanna stick my dick in her one more time, at least."

"Abe, we have to get her away from Black Nile Industries as soon as possible. If what you say about her and Mercee is true, then the problem is more severe than we ever realized. We've been reviewing the records in the operating system under the belief that Mercee has been hiding orders. But if Nysha is involved, she could have very well recoded the whole operating system itself, where every illicit thing they do would process automatically, without effort or even a trace of transgression."

"I don't wanna let her off the hook, Nick; no, that's not what I'm saying. I want her to pay for messing with my shit. I just don't wanna shoot her in the head yet. But I do want her to feel a little bit of pain."

"How much pain?"

"I wanna see blood," I say. "Lots of it. And I don't want her to see it coming."

UP NEXT:

Hush Love 3

Text JORDAN to 77948

And stay updated on all of Jordan Belcher Presents' *newest releases, free giveaways,* and *special promotions!*

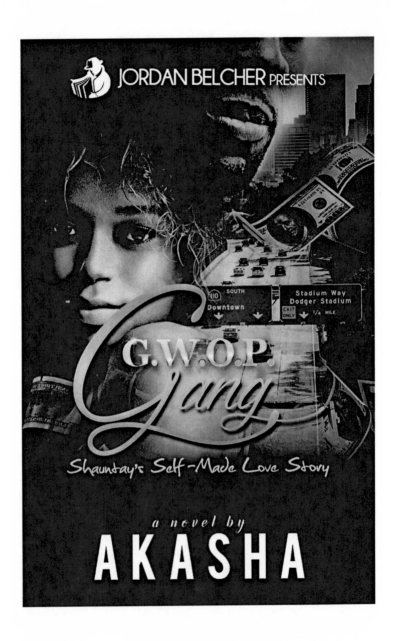

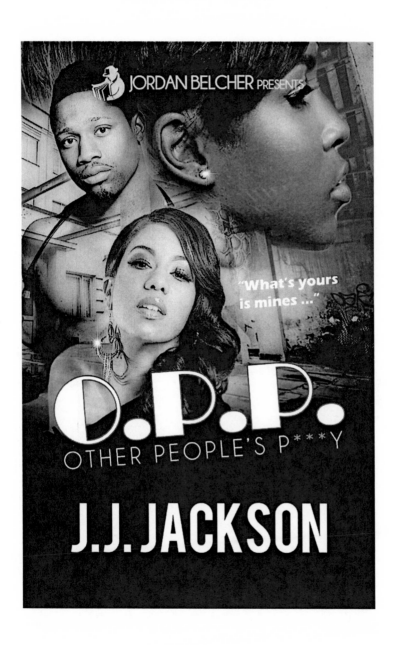

CPSIA information can be obtained
at www.ICGtesting.com
Printed in the USA
LVOW12s1540150217
524373LV00001B/234/P